I0663815

# DEATH BY MOONLIGHT

MAGNOLIA BLUFF CRIME CHRONICLES
BOOK 32

C W HAWES

CWH BOOKS

## ENTER THE IMAGINATIVE WORLD OF CW HAWES

Enter my world and you'll find that murder was never so good. Just click, tap, or scan the QR code below.

There's nothing like a good old-fashioned slow burn murder mystery. The quirky characters. The eccentric sleuth. The bumbling police detectives. The nefarious villain. And of course, the leisurely pacing until we reach the exciting climax.

If you are new to the Magnolia Bluff Crime Chronicles, then *Death By Moonlight* is an excellent entry point into the series and into my world.

In addition to my books in the Magnolia Bluff Crime Chronicles, I write the Justinia Wright Private Investigator Mysteries, which are an homage to Nero Wolfe and Archie Goodwin. You'll discover exciting stories, eccentric and quirky characters, and wicked killers. And if you like Magnolia Bluff, you're sure to like Justinia Wright's Minneapolis.

So just click, tap, or scan the QR code to enter my exciting world of mystery and mayhem. You will get a free copy of *Vampire*

*House and Other Early Cases of Justinia Wright, PI* and you'll get my monthly email of news and curated contact. The game is a foot!

Book Cover Design: Wyldwood Books

Created with Vellum

*To the memory Caleb Pirtle III*
*author, mentor, friend, brother*

# PROLOGUE

WHAT I'M HEARING IS PRETTY close to the sound of silence. No cars about. The birds are still asleep, although most of them have moved further south.

If one is especially quiet, the distant low of a cow can be heard drifting in the wind. It's a plaintive sound. Better, though, than the eerie cry of a coyote.

The Green is empty. I half expected to see Fergus, the sometime town drunk, or Graham Huston, the newspaper editor. The temperature must be too cold for Fergus, and Graham must not be in one of his pensive moods. I guess I'm being pensive for him.

I've been up since Maximilian and Monette's 2 AM feeding. They are the gifts Ember and I received on Christmas day. Not being able to get back to sleep, I got dressed and walked to downtown.

The bench across from my shop, the Really Good Wood-Fired Coffee and Ice Cream Emporium, was empty, and here I sit, smoking my pipe. Taking Graham's pensive place.

My name, by the way, is Harry Thurgood. I moved to Magnolia Bluff several years ago. It's a good place to live. Most of the time. If you don't factor in the murders, that is.

Murders aside, I like it here. I love the Texas Hill Country. And I love the antics of small town busy-bodies.

Ah, that cow again. There were no cows where I'm originally from. Just ostentatious piles, walls, gates, asphalt streets, concrete sidewalks, and lots of green lawn and stately trees. And money. Can't forget the money.

Magnolia Bluff has those people, my family's people. They live up on Sandalwood Drive. I don't live there. I guess I'm not entirely my family's people anymore.

When Em realized she was pregnant, I bought a house, an old house, built by a rail baron just outside the city limits. We've updated the old structure without altering its heritage, and made it a good place to raise a family.

I confess I have no knowledge of the history of Magnolia Bluff. But I do occasionally wonder where towns come from in general and my town specifically.

Accident? Design? Convenience? Necessity?

And why was our town called Magnolia Bluff? No bluffs here. And no magnolia trees either. At least not native. Did the name serve as a reminder of where he came from? What he was leaving behind? Or running from?

I don't know. And there are too many conflicting myths today to try to sort it all out.

What I do know is that this place is now my home. I am not a native Texan, but I am proud to be called a Texan. I hope Emmy can stay here. She's the Methodist minister and nothing is guaranteed for Methodist ministers. They are up for review every year.

Some of those busybodies I mentioned earlier are making life very difficult for her and, by extension, me as well. So nothing is guaranteed. As they say, if wishes were horses, beggars would ride.

I'm not a religious guy. If there is a god, I believe he helps those who help themselves. But Emmy believes Jesus talks to her. I hope she can convince him to let her stay. Because wherever she goes, I will follow. She is the love of my life. How could I do otherwise?

Now you're probably itching to get this story started. So I'm going to let you do just that. But just so you're aware, I'm largely telling the story. Although there will be parts that are not from my point of view. They've been added after the fact, so to speak, to form a cohesive whole. My editor decided it would be best that way.

And now, since my pipe is out, turn the page and we'll get started.

# 1

## FOUR MONTHS AGO

SERGEANT INVESTIGATOR REECE SOVERN knocked on the police chief's door.

When he heard, "Come in," he entered and said, "You wanted to see me?"

"Ah, yes. Have a seat, Reece."

He sat in the straight-backed dark oak chair across the desk from Chief Jager.

"Got a call from the state AG's office about twenty minutes ago asking me to cooperate with you and assist you in any way I can, should you ask. Do you want to tell me what this is all about?"

"You spoke with the AG?"

"His assistant." Jager's look expected an answer and no beating around the bush.

Reece took a deep breath and exhaled. "I'm working undercover for the attorney general and the state senate's ethics committee."

"Seriously?"

Reece nodded and pushed his glasses back to the top of his nose.

"Why you?"

Reece was aware of what Tommy was thinking: *How can a mostly incompetent boob get the attention of the attorney general?* To the chief, he said, "Not sure. Got a conference call from the AG himself and the committee chairman requesting my services to investigate state senators who are suspected of abusing their positions."

"When was this?"

"Back in January."

"And you didn't tell me?"

"Was told that since I would be operating undercover, it would be best if no one knew. Didn't even breathe a word to my dog."

Tommy chuckled. "I see. Were you investigating Senator David when those foreigners were here?"

"Yes."

"So you weren't actually trying to help him?"

Reece smiled. "Help him get caught."

"Which he did. But you made it look like..." The chief gave him the squint eye.

"I was a bumbling incompetent. Yes. Hetta keeps telling me I should try out for community theater."

"Well, I'll be damned."

"I'll admit I don't have the big city experience of Turner. And I'll even confess to the rumors that I lack imagination. But I'm an honest cop and I don't easily give up. Plus, I'm trying to take a page out of Thurgood's book to be more observant."

"I don't know what to say."

"You don't need to say anything. I should let you know the AG has made arrangements for me to get FBI training."

"Are you going to Washington?"

"No. The AG said they were sending a trainer here."

"Well, I'll be..." Jager shook his head and stood. "I suppose I can't say anything either."

"Probably not."

The chief nodded his head. "Okay. Just say the word if I can help."

"I will, Chief."

Reece left and headed to his office. *I may not be the best, but I'm good enough that someone requests my help and tosses in top-notch training to boot.*

Entering his little eight-by-eight domain, Reece grabbed his topcoat and hat off the tree. He took the Zeppelin cigar pipe out of his pocket and clenched it with his teeth.

"I think I will go down to the Really Good and get one of Harry's fancy coffees. Have a little celebration. The shock on Tommy's face. Wish I had a picture."

# 2

## THE PRESENT

Thursday, January 9, 4:38 pm

THE CLOUDS HAD HUNG low in the sky all day. A dark gray ceiling dropping drizzle every now and again. Which probably explains the run we had on the chili, broccoli cheddar soup, and hot roast beef sandwiches. And probably not surprising no one was interested in frozen custard.

Quite a few large coffees went out the door, and quite a few cups were lingered over at the tables.

Since marrying Ember Cole, the Methodist minister, and joining St. Luke's United Methodist Church, I've seen a steady increase in local traffic. I guess it pays to be churched in small town Texas.

By quarter to four the tables were empty, although Charmaine Adler did stop in for a chamomile tea with soy milk to go. I managed an upsell. She also left with a slice of tomato basil bread topped with a thick layer of brown olive relish.

How she juggled all of that in her BMW SUV, I have no idea.

I'd have spilled coffee and the bread would've ended up on the upholstery, relish side down.

Charmaine was the last paying customer of the day, because Graham Huston doesn't count. He doesn't pay for anything.

Graham became the owner and editor of the *Magnolia Bluff Chronicle,* our newspaper, when Neal Holland, the former editor, was murdered.

The paper doesn't make much money. Enough though that Graham usually has two nickels to rub together. He rents a room from Nell Walker, who has a three-room boarding house behind the high school football field.

Before I got married, he'd show up after closing hours for dinner and we'd ponder the way of the world, along with living and loving in Magnolia Bluff. We never came to any conclusions, but that's how those kinds of discussions go.

Now, he usually gets dinner to go. Once in a while I stay and we philosophize like we did in the old days.

Today he came in at four thirty-eight to pick up his supper. I handed him the bag.

"Here you go Graham. One bowl of chili, Yankee style. Cornbread. Packets of honey. A hot roast beef sandwich. And four cream cheese kolaches. Anything else?"

"No. That will be plenty. How much do I owe you? And don't give me any crap about it being your turn to pay."

"I do believe it is my turn."

"You said that yesterday *and* the day before that *and* the day before that. Now, how much is it?"

Before I could answer, he turned to Jack Bonhoffer, my floor manager, who also mans the cash register, and said, "How much is this Jack?"

"Don't take his money," I told Jack. "He was printing it earlier today. The ink will probably smear."

"One of these days, Harry, I'm going to come in here when you're not around and stuff a bunch of bills in that cash register."

"Monika likes a paycheck. She told me herself. And Landon needs one for that wife and baby he has. And I don't think you want Nell throwing you out in the rain."

"Okay. I get your point. I just don't like feeling that I'm a mooch."

"You're not. Just a friend helping a friend. Can't I help a friend?"

"All right, Harry. You win this round. Thanks for the grub. I appreciate it."

"Bon appetite, mon ami."

Graham left and missed by ten minutes the oddest spectacle of the day.

# 3

## THURSDAY, JANUARY 9, 4:52 PM

I'D JUST FINISHED WIPING down the counter, Jack was counting the day's take, and Estrelita, my waitress, was wiping down tables.

Miguel, my cook, was in the kitchen and the thwack of the cleaver cutting chickens apart sounded through the open window between the kitchen and the rest of the coffee shop.

Only eight minutes to go before I flipped the sign from open to closed and put the Really Good Wood-Fired Coffee and Ice Cream Emporium to bed for the night.

The bell over the door sounded. A man entered and stopped. He stood in the doorway and I watched his head turn and his eyes take in the empty tables and chairs.

Estrelita and Jack stopped what they were doing and stared at the man. Only the sound of Miguel's cleaver filled the silence.

The fellow was tall and broad shouldered. His torso and arms looked substantial. The two-piece black suit was tight around his body. A lot of muscle and bulk there. His shirt was white, the top button was unbuttoned. No necktie. There was a gold chain instead. Black tennis shoes were on his feet. In his ear lobes were black spacers with a diamond in the center that glinted in the light from the ceiling fixtures.

The stranger's mirrored sunglasses turned in my direction.

He strode to the counter, took a photo out of the inside suit coat pocket and placed it before me.

"Have you seen this person?"

His voice was the crunch of car tires on gravel.

My eyes dropped to the photo. It was of a pretty girl, but no one I recognized. I looked at the man, eyeballs to sunglasses.

"No, I haven't. Does she live here?"

"I was hoping you'd tell me."

He repeated the performance with Estrelita and Jack, and got negatives from both.

He thrust his chin towards the kitchen window. "Ask him."

I took the picture, had Miguel look at it, and got another negative.

"Sorry," I said when I handed the picture back to him.

"I'm at that motel, south end of town. Room six. If you see her."

"Will do."

He strode from the shop, and I watched him cross East Main Street, the Green, West Main, get into a black Suburban parked on West Main, and drive off.

"That was strange," Jack said.

"That it was," I responded.

"She's a pretty girl," Estrelita said. "I wonder who she is."

"Perhaps a sister," I said. "There's a certain resemblance to Mr. Sunglasses."

"At least he didn't want something to eat," Jack said.

"There is that," I replied. "It was strange, though."

Miguel's cleaver thunked into the cutting board.

*I hope that isn't an omen.*

I flipped the sign from open to closed.

# 4

## THURSDAY, JANUARY 9, 5:29 PM

I PULLED into the long driveway and stopped the Alfa Romeo before one of the five garage doors.

In the parking area off the circle, I noticed my old BMW, which I'd given to Jearlene Reston. Apparently, she was working late.

I'd hired her to be our housekeeper and cook. Monday through Friday. The pay I'd offered was much better than what the internet company was paying, so she said yes immediately. And because she was a widow with young children, more money was better.

I crossed the hundred feet to the front door, and thought, as I often did since buying this old place, that the chauffeur would've dropped me off at the front door and gone on to park the car. And probably the butler, or a footman, would've opened the door for me.

Nowadays, we rich folk do all this ourselves. How the mighty have fallen.

Using my key, I unlocked the door and entered my little mansion.

The hundred bulbs in the crystal chandelier were not lit. Only the wall sconces illuminated the grand foyer. And they were enough. The light bounced off the white walls, gleamed on the polished dark wood floors, and illuminated the grand spiral staircase.

A spectacular home to show off one's wealth. Which was, of course, why the railroad magnate built it.

I deposited hat and coat in the closet and heard whining behind the door to the library. The sound of my new Hovawart pup, Princess. No ordinary dog for this guy. No sirree Bob. I had to get one of the rarest dog breeds in America.

A turn of the knob, and a push on the door, and there she was dancing all around me.

Kneeling on the hardwood floor, I put my arms around her, endured her kisses, hugged her, and asked, "Were you a good girl today? Did you protect your family?"

She nuzzled in close, and taking that for a yes, I asked her where Ember was.

Immediately, she stopped her wiggling and cuddling, dashed into the library, stopped and turned her head.

"I'm coming. Go on."

I followed her through the library and into the family room, where my bride was sitting by the fire nursing the babies.

"Hi, Harry. I knew you were home because Princess's ears suddenly perked up, then I heard the door open. How are you?"

I gave Em a kiss, said, "Wonderful, now that I see you," and sat on the loveseat on the other side of the fireplace across from her.

"This feels good. Rather chill out there."

"A dreary, drizzly winter day."

"That it is."

"How was your day?"

"Business was pretty good. Also approved two loans for a couple of house flippers."

"That hard money lending idea has sure paid off."

"I'm surprised at how well it's paid off. And the two defaults netted us a couple of properties with great potential. Gunther Fight, eat your heart out."

Em giggled. "I bet some very un-Christian words are being said about you."

"Probably. How was your day?"

"You know, Harry, I'm getting bored. You hired a nanny for these little gems. And Clara's wonderful, don't get me wrong, and I'm grateful you thought to hire one so I can carry on my ministry. I'm also thankful you hired Jearlene to be our housekeeper and cook. And *she's* very grateful. She tells me at least once a day. The problem is I have nothing to do."

"If you're tired of reading the complete works of John Wesley and have had your fill of bonbons and reality TV, cut your maternity leave short and climb back into the saddle."

"I suppose I can, but…"

"But what? Clara will take care of Max and Netty."

"Are you really going to call her that?"

I lifted my shoulders and let them fall. "Sure. Why not? What's the eye roll for?"

"You. Yes, Clara can take care of the twins, and I can pump milk so she can feed them while I'm gone."

"So, what's the problem?"

"Nothing, I guess."

"I know Waymon Riggins, Euel Pinckney, Maness Sebren, and the rest of those twats will welcome you back with open arms. Especially Reverend Humphrey."

"You are incorrigible, Mister. You know that?"

"I suppose I do. But, just sayin', pick your poison."

"Probably not wise to say that out loud here in Magnolia Bluff."

"Except we're just over the city line, which makes us not in the city."

"Oh, so that makes a difference, does it?"

"One can hope."

Jearlene Reston appeared in the doorway. "Hello, Mr. Thurgood."

"Hi, Jerri. Everything okay?"

"Yes, it is. Your dinner is ready any time you are. It's on the warmers and in the oven. I'm going home now."

"Thanks, Jerri, and I'll see you tomorrow. Lord willing," Em said.

"Yes, Lord willing. Goodnight."

Jerri left, and I asked Em if I should call for Clara to take the twins.

"No need, sir. I was just going to check with the Reverend to see if they were done nursing."

"You must have ESP or something," I said.

"A body just knows, sir."

"You're aware of them and you don't even see them," I said, and added, "I, on the other hand, wouldn't even have a clue looking at them."

She smiled and looked at Em. "Are they done, Reverend?"

"Max is. Monette is sleeping and using me for a pacifier, I think."

"They do that sometimes, ma'am. If you're ready?"

Ember kissed each baby's head and then handed them to Clara, who then presented them to me for goodnight kisses, which I gladly gave. Then they were off to the upstairs bedroom.

"Come on," I said, "let's see what Jerri prepared for us."

Em stood. "You know, Harry—"

"I think I do."

"Oh, man, that deserves an eye roll."

I flashed her a grin. "I suppose so. Sorry for interrupting."

She playfully swatted my behind. "No, you're not. Anyway, I was thinking how life is pretty quiet for us now. We're settled into a comfortable and pleasant routine. And I like that."

"You aren't forgetting about the guy who tried to burn down the Really Good, are you? Or getting saddled with a Mary Lousponsored assistant pastor? Or Wilbur's first month with Princess? Or—"

"Okay, I get your point, Mister. And thanks for bursting my bubble. But let me add that Reece hasn't been by to arrest us recently, and in spite of the Reverend Adelbert Humphrey the fourth things have been pretty quiet at church. And Adelbert's worked out surprisingly well. He's twenty-eight going on eighty and the old ladies seem to love him. Which will allow me to focus on the college as soon as I get back to work."

"I guess you have a point. Things have been going well since our last arrest and you coming out of the closet to tell the world you were a pornstar and a prostitute who ditched the sex life for the Christ life."

Ember was shaking her head.

"What?"

"You would have to mention that, wouldn't you?"

I grinned at her. "Just sayin'."

"Well, quit sayin'. I'm not proud of that phase of my life."

"Okay. Sorry. You're right, though, things have been moving along quite swimmingly."

"What are you doing?"

"Touching wood. Now that I've mentioned how good life has been, I don't want to jinx things."

# 5

## THURSDAY, JANUARY 9, 8:01 PM

MARY LOU FIGHT stood by the fireplace in the day room of her home and took in the fifteen women sitting on the chairs and sofas before her.

Seated next to her on her right was Oralene Fight, formerly Oralene Reston, Mary Lou's adopted daughter.

To Mary Lou's left was seated Pearline Applewhite, who kept stealing surreptitious glances at Oralene.

The women all wore crimson hats of diverse shapes and sizes. All wore yellow feather boas around their necks. And everyone was clad in purple dresses of various shades and hues.

Mary Lou spoke. "Come to order, please. The New Order of the Crimson Hat Society is now in session, and it is my good pleasure to welcome back into membership Charmaine Adler. Mrs. Adler was a member of the original Crimson Hat Society, and now she has joined our new society. Please welcome her."

Reserved applause rippled through the room, and stopped when Mary Lou raised her white gloved hand.

"A new year is upon us," she began, "and I have decided that new tactics are in order. Reverend Cole still holds the pastorate of Saint Luke's United Methodist Church. And what's more, she is living in common law sin with that unscrupulous and deviously cunning lothario, Harry Thurgood, if that's even his real name.

"To this point, they have survived every attempt I have made to remove them from our city. They have not only survived, but have thrived. And in each instance, they emerge even more well-liked by the mindless and immoral hoi polloi who control our town.

"Therefore, we will change our approach. You will join me on my return to Saint Luke's. I intend to become active once more in the life of my church, the church where I was baptized. And you all will as well."

"But, but we all have our own churches," Violet Granger said.

Mary Lou watched Violet shrink under her gaze. "Mrs. Granger, who gave you permission to interrupt your queen? Hm?"

"Uh, no one, my Queen."

"That is correct. No one. And certainly not I, your Queen. I will think of a suitable punishment in due time. You have been warned.

"Now, everyone who is not a member of Saint Luke's will immediately apply for membership. The Reverend Miss Cole wants new members, so she shall have them. She shall have you."

"My Queen," Oralene began, "this is a brilliant plan. More members on our side means more votes. More votes to thwart the strumpet and cast her out of God's house."

"That is true, my daughter. I am pleased you recognize the brilliance of my plan. In a moment, Eliška will serve refreshments."

Mary Lou sat and surveyed the murmuring women.

*Every one of these women has a secret that they do not want made public, which allows me to turn them to my will. And when I've strategically placed them in my church, the strumpet will fall.*

*Her reign of godlessness will be over and I will once again control my church. What's more, once I have my church under control, then I will get my city under control and throw out the commoners and heathen. Magnolia Bluff will then be purified.*

# 6

## THURSDAY, JANUARY 9, 8:37 PM

WE LEISURELY DISPOSED of Jerri's fried chicken, squash casserole, biscuits, pan-fried okra with cornmeal, and apple pie while talking about nothing in particular.

With full bellies, we took ourselves back to the family room. I tossed a couple of logs on the bed of hot coals, made myself a Corpse Reviver No. 1, and picked up where I left off in Caleb Pirtle's chronicle of the town of Borger, Texas.

Emmy was drinking jasmine-scented green tea and reading a spiritualist novel by Cindy Davis. Wilbur was in her lap. I suppose taking advantage of the twins not being there.

Princess was curled up on the hearthrug, soaking up the heat.

I love fireplaces, and had insisted that the furniture be arranged so that we and any guests sat by the fire.

Directly opposite the fireplace are Ember's and my wing-backs, with a table between us. Two loveseats face each other, with a coffee table in between, which fills in the space between us and the fire. Forming a box, so to speak, in front of the flames.

We were both smoking our pipes when she suddenly said, "I think I'm going to have to go on a diet."

I puffed on my old briar a couple of times before asking her why.

"This pipe tobacco got me thinking," she said. "It's so sweet. Like dessert."

"Pipe tobacco is going to make you go on a diet?"

"No, silly. First Miguel and now Jerri. They don't cook waistline friendly food. It's all rich and filled with fat and loads of calories. Then I got all fat with the twins, and now that they are out, I'm still pudgy. And all of that southern-fried goodness isn't helping me to get rid of the pudgies. Before you know it, I'm going to look like a beach ball. I just know I am."

I puffed on my pipe and thought a moment before answering. And when I did, I kept my eyes on my book and casually said, "Just as long as you don't roll so fast I can't catch you."

"Gee, thanks, Mister. And what happens if you catch me?"

I looked at her. "Well, you know. Maybe a younger brother or sister for the twins."

"You want more kids?"

"Sure. Why not? We can afford them."

"Can I wear shoes?"

"What? You don't like being barefoot?"

"No. They have hookworm in the south."

"Then shoed and pregnant is fine with me."

Emmy leaned back in the chair, drank tea, puffed on her pipe, left hand rubbing the area where Max and Netty had recently been. Wilbur jumped down and transferred to the back of the loveseat in front of her.

"You truly want more children?"

"You don't?"

I watched the "I'm thinking" look descend on her face for a moment and then lift. She said, "I guess that's okay. Will you still love me if I'm fat?"

A big smile spread across my face. "Of course. I'll love you whatever your shape. I will love you when you're old and wrinkled and bent with arthritis. You are the one I love, Ember Cole, and I will continue to love you when death parts us. I-love-*you*."

She reached out her hand, and I took it. "I love you, Harry

Thurgood. Every day, I thank God for bringing you into my life. I thank Him for your unwavering faithfulness while I sorted things out in my head. Thank you, my love, for waiting for me. Thank you for the joy you bring to me. I am totally yours."

"You were worth waiting for."

She tilted her head up and focused on the ceiling, roughly where our bedroom was, then those beautiful eyes focused on mine.

There was a glow in her eyes and a huskiness to her voice. "You want to get in some practice for pregnancy number two?"

"Start rolling, little ball, because I'm going to catch you."

"Gee, thanks, Mister. Little ball. Sheesh."

Then she jumped out of her chair and took off running, yelling, "Catch me if you can!"

Princess was up and running after her, and I was not far behind.

Wilbur's head poked up and then returned to the soft sofa.

# 7

## FRIDAY, JANUARY 10, 6:30 AM

ANOTHER MORNING in beautiful Magnolia Bluff, Texas. The air was crisp. Potato chip crisp. The moisture from your breath made you look like you were steam powered, or a whale coming up for air.

I dressed casually today.

Dark chocolate slacks. The ninety percent cacao dark chocolate.

A white shirt. Snow white, even though we're experiencing drizzle and not snow.

Instead of a tie, a brown and gold ascot with a dark red pattern flowing through it.

A dark tan camel-hair sport coat topped it off.

For the weather, I donned a deep burgundy, almost black raincoat and skipped my normal pork pie for a Tilley TTW2 TecWool hat. It is the ultimate winter headgear.

Once I'd reached the shop, the raincoat and hat took up residence in the tiny office off the kitchen.

Miguel was busy slicing tomatoes. Estrelita was checking tables to make sure they had the condiments patrons often requested. Jack Bonhoffer was sitting at the cash register waiting for the paying customers. And I was making a final check of the day's menu.

At 6:30, I flipped the sign from closed to open and unlocked the door. Another day at the Really Good Wood-Fired Coffee and Ice Cream Emporium had begun.

My eyes swept the Green and both Main Streets and there it was. Parked in front of the bank. The big black Suburban.

Why was it there at this hour of the morning? Was the guy a Fed after all and yesterday's performance a ruse?

My mind went back to my last art sale. Every time I make one, a tiny part of me wonders if the buyer is a plant. Even though I have a rigorous vetting process, it's possible an agent might slip through. No system is perfect.

The buyer was a wealthy Chinese businessman. Sort of an oxymoron in a Communist society. At least in theory. In practice? The rich survive and thrive no matter the politics.

He answered my advertisement on the Dark Web and wanted to buy the painting that technically didn't exist.

In reality, the work of art had been rescued from the flames that were cleansing the Reich of degenerate art. Although that was mostly anti-Nazi propaganda. In truth, the National Socialists sold most of the degenerate art to degenerate collectors and museums outside of Germany to raise money for the Reich.

The Germans. They're smart people.

The painting the Communist billionaire bought had been stored in an attic until American troops liberated it.

It was subsequently "lost" again when the Army shipped the painting to the United States.

The sale had gone off without a hitch. The piece of art was taken possession of by the businessman's agent and I received 13.8 million dollars. Half in cash. The other half in gold.

In the business I'm in, you don't want to get the banks involved. They're mandatory reporters. Thank you organized crime.

If the agent had been a Fed, the moment I touched that money, it would have been the big house for this guy.

Which means I'm worrying over nothing. Mr. Sunglasses is probably exactly who he appears to be: some guy looking for a woman.

The bell over the door took me out of my musings. Fergus shambled in out of the cold and wet.

"Mornin' Mr. Thurgood. Be careful. The eyes are watching. They're looking. They're observing. Watch for the eyes. Mornin' Miss Estrelita."

"Good morning, Mr. Fergus," she replied. A smile was on her face and in her voice. "Would you like coffee?"

"Yes, ma'am. Hot and black."

I watched the old vet shuffle over to the table in the corner. He sat with his back against the wall.

Estrelita brought him his coffee.

Fergus has always been a puzzle to me.

He has this mystical sage air about him, yet when I came to Magnolia Bluff he was the town drunk. Mystical sage or not.

Then he was given a place to stay in the Woman's Building and he seemed to be on the road to recovery and a normal life.

All that changed when the Woman's Building burned down and he was injured. That brought back the PTSD and God knows what other trauma. Once again, four walls became intolerable and the bottle a comfort. And that I got straight from the old guy himself.

So here I am again, playing the good Samaritan and giving him a free breakfast and coffee every morning except Sunday. The Really Good isn't open on Sundays. Often, though, there's a bag by the front door with his name on it.

I took a seat at his table.

"So, what's this about the eyes?"

"You don't know?"

"If I did, I wouldn't be asking."

He nodded. His rheumy and bloodshot eyes scanned my face.

"That door to your closet isn't going to stay closed forever, Mr. Thurgood. Not if you plan on staying in Magnolia Bluff."

"You think I have a closet full of skeletons?"

"Who doesn't? Even Mary Lou Fight has her closet." He drank coffee. "But the moat can be crossed, the portcullis smashed, and the doors battered down. Can they not?"

I favored him with a smile. "With enough persistence."

He returned the smile. But his contained no mirth. None at all. "There are some in this town who have more persistence than Edison."

Estrelita brought his food and asked if he wanted anything else. He said no, while reaching for the salt and pepper, and she left.

"Thanks for the advice. I appreciate it. I'll leave you to your breakfast."

"You aren't going to heed it, are you?"

"I'm considering my best course of action."

"Don't think too long, Mr. Thurgood. There are eyes everywhere. They're watching. And they never blink."

His eyes turned to his food, and I made my way back to my table in the opposite corner, grabbing a coffee and two raised glazed doughnuts en route.

I sat and studied the old vet while he ate.

*What does he actually know?*

*How much is just a guess based on snippets he hears here and there?*

*How much is a bad dream from too much booze and bad pizza snatched from the dumpster behind Olivia's?*

*And is that guy a Fed after all?*

# 8

## FRIDAY, JANUARY 10, 8:14 AM

CAPTAIN DAVIS ANTHONY BRIGGS of the Magnolia Bluff police department took a sip of coffee, raised his eyebrows, and set the cup down.

*Sovern wasn't kidding when he said the Really Good's coffee was a little bit of heaven on earth. I've no idea why it took me this long to try it.*

He bit into the cream cheese kolache and his eyes opened wide. *As good as Aunt Lizzie's. Maybe better. I'll have to tell Sovern thanks for bugging me to visit Thurgood's shop.*

There was a knock on the door.

"Come in."

The door opened and in walked the chief of the MBPD.

Briggs started to rise, but noticed the hand signal to remain seated. He settled back into his chair.

The Chief sat in the chair on the opposite side of the desk.

"Well, Davis, you've been here for two entire months in our lovely town. What's your impression?"

"Okay by me, Chief. A lot quieter than Bozeman. What's the smile for?"

"You've been lucky. You've read through our past cases?"

"Yes, sir. You seem to have had more than your fair share of violent crime over the past three years."

"Possibly."

"And you seem to rely on civilians. A lot. A bit unorthodox, that, isn't it?"

The Chief shrugged. "What can I say? We do catch the bad guys."

"I suppose. Still..."

"Perhaps we won't need to rely on civilians now that you're here. We can benefit from someone with city experience."

"I believe my experience will be a definite help, sir."

"Good. Because that's why I hired you." The Chief stood. "We had a quiet Christmas and so far a quiet beginning to the year. Let's hope it stays that way."

"Yes, sir. Better to have quiet days than busy days."

"That it is."

Briggs watched the door close behind his boss. His eyes shifted to the sheet of paper on which he'd been listing names, and he pulled it to the center of his desk.

While he drank coffee and ate kolaches, he scanned the names he'd written on the paper.

Harry Thurgood
Rev. Ember Cole
Graham Huston
Monika Crow
Bliss Jager
Dr. Mike Kurelek
Caroline McCluskey
Magnolia Nadine Roane
Brandon Turner
Blue Bonet
Gloria McBride

. . .

He set his coffee mug down. *Those people have repeatedly elbowed their way into police investigations, and one, Brandon Turner, was asked to assist by the Chief himself. The Sheriff's CID unit should've been brought in.*

"This has got to stop," Briggs said out loud before picking up his mug and taking a sip of coffee. "Under my watch, there will be *no* civilian interlopers in *any* police business."

He set the mug down and picked up a kolache and took a bite. After he'd chewed and swallowed, he continued his monologue to himself.

"I will see to it that any civilian interfering in police business will be arrested and charged with every single chargeable offense in the book."

# 9

## FRIDAY, JANUARY 10, 9:46 AM

LARRILYN HAMMER, the receptionist and secretary at Saint Luke's United Methodist Church, knocked on the door and poked her head into Ember's office.

"Oralene Fight is here to see you."

"Thank you, Larrilyn. How do these people know I'm here?"

"Uh..."

"Never mind. It was a rhetorical question. Give me a minute and then send her in."

When Larrilyn's head disappeared, Ember felt herself deflate.

*Now what? I come in to catch up on mail and check with Adelbert about Sunday's service and instead find myself drowning in Crimson Hats wanting to join the church. And now little Mary Lou shows up. What next?*

The door opened and in walked Oralene Fight. "Good morning, Reverend Cole."

"Good morning, Miss Fight. How may I help you?"

Ember watched the young woman's eyes roam the office.

*One thing's for certain,* Ember said to herself, *this young woman has ambition. And knows how to manipulate people to get what she wants. But how she got herself into Mary Lou's good graces is beyond me.*

"A lot could be done with this office," Oralene said. "When it is Bertie's, I will make sure it is..." Her eyes caught Ember's. "Not so austere."

Ember stood. "I would love to help you daydream. However, I do have work to do. So if you don't mind?"

"Work?" Oralene, rather primly, sat in a chair on the other side of Ember's desk. Her back was very straight. "I thought you were on maternity leave. Tired of children already? Hm?"

"No, I'm not tired of my children. You see, young lady, I can only eat so many bonbons a day. I don't wish to tire of them. And as for the simplicity of my office, it helps remind me of how our Lord lived. I am now a wealthy woman. I don't wish to let my blessing become a curse. Mr. Thurgood—"

"Your *common-law* husband?"

Ember could feel the sneer roll off her adversary as if it were the heat off of a wildfire. She ignored it and sat. Her eyes took in Oralene's face. *As lovely as an angel. As devious as a devil.*

"Yes, that is true. We chose the common law route. I suppose there are people here who regard Adam and Eve, along with the Patriarchs and their wives, as fornicators because they didn't get a blessing from a Christian minister."

"Were you a fornicator or an adulteress performing sex acts in front of a camera?"

"I was a sinner who was and is saved by grace."

"Ah, yes. Perhaps you should have changed your name to Joanna Newton."

"Perhaps, but I didn't. I was going to share a bit of wisdom with you, but obviously you'd rather sit here and cast stones. Although, as I recall, your own house is made of glass. Is it not?"

Ember saw a bit of color rise to Oralene's cheeks, and smiled to herself, while keeping her face deadpan for her visitor.

Oralene cleared her throat. "I'm sorry. I interrupted you."

"I was going to say Mr. Thurgood is fond of quoting from Seneca's *On the Happy Life* when the discussion turns to wealth."

From the blank look on the young woman's face, Ember

knew she had no idea who Seneca was. And neither had she until she'd met Harry.

Ember smiled inwardly at her good fortune at having met him.

"And what does this Seneca say about wealth?"

Ember recited from memory. "For the wise man does not consider himself unworthy of any gifts from Fortune's hands; he does not love wealth but he would rather have it; he does not admit it into his heart but into his home; and what wealth is his he does not reject but keeps, wishing it to supply greater scope for him to practice his virtue. For the wise man regards wealth as a slave, the fool as a master."

"Was this Seneca a saint?"

"The early Christians thought so. But no, he wasn't. He was a Stoic philosopher."

"I see."

And Ember could tell from her face that no, she didn't.

"So Miss Fight, I appreciate the social call. However, I do have a bit more to do before it's feeding time for my babies."

Oralene rose from her chair, and Ember thought she did so gracefully.

"You'll make sure my application for membership is processed quickly?"

"I have no control over that. The Membership Committee, though, will review it as soon as possible, I'm sure."

"Good. Thank you, Reverend Cole. A good morning to you."

"And to you, Miss Fight."

Ember watched Oralene leave; and after she was gone, got up and closed the office door.

She returned to her desk. "Lord, please forgive me for what I am about to do. But even Elisha, by Your power, struck down those who taunted him."

Ember dialed a number on her cell phone. "Hello, Rosalind? This is Ember Cole."

"Good morning, Pastor.

"Good morning. I hope the day finds you well."

"It does, thank you. How are the little ones?"

"All they do is eat and sleep."

"That is all they do at first. Just you wait, though. The fun is coming."

"So they tell me. I have a question."

"Okay. Ask."

"Something is going on. I think Mary Lou is up to some new shenanigans."

"Not surprised. What is it this time?"

"I've had four Crimson Hats in this morning—"

"Are you at the office? I thought you were on maternity leave."

"Yes, to both. I just had to get out of the house for a couple of hours and do some work. I'm beginning to feel like a cow."

Rosalind laughed. "And reality TV isn't doing it for you either."

"Oh, my God. I have no idea how people can watch that stuff. Anyway, I've had four Hats in applying for membership."

"Wait a minute. Say what?"

"Four Hats want to become members, plus Oralene was in asking about her membership request. May the Lord forgive me, but is there any way you can slow down the process?"

Rosalind laughed. "Could Jael drive a tent peg? You leave it to me. I'll find some red tape. I suppose those Hats are already churched."

"That they are."

"All right. Leave it to me."

"Thank you, Rosalind."

"Don't you worry none, Pastor. We'll find a way to see what's underneath the sheepskin. Goodbye."

Ember said goodbye and ended the call.

She drummed her fingers on her desk pad. "I wonder if the Queen has finally decided to return?"

# 10

## FRIDAY, JANUARY 10, 11:02 AM

THE REALLY GOOD was moderately busy. Moderately busy for the Really Good, that is.

Eleven people occupied four tables and two men sat at the counter.

While drafting new advertising copy for the *Chronicle,* I was keeping my eye on things in case Estrelita needed a helping hand.

The bell over the door rang and I looked up to see who'd entered. Two women were standing in the doorway. They were holding hands and wet umbrellas. And from the look of their coats and hats, they'd just time portaled from the Edwardian era.

I didn't recall seeing them about town, at least in that attire. Then again, with ten thousand people in Magnolia Bluff there's bound to be someone you don't know or haven't seen.

Their eyes swept the shop and stopped when they saw me. They smiled and crossed the floor to my table. I stood to greet them.

"Hello, ladies. How may I help you?"

The taller of the two, who had a gorgeous shade of red hair under the hat, said, "Are you Harry Thurgood?"

"I am, and who do I have the pleasure of addressing?"

The taller one answered. "I am Augustinia Faber and this is my cousin and wife, Hester Galt. We have been given to understand that you are a moneylender."

"I'm a hard asset lender, yes. Have a seat. You may put your umbrellas and coats on that table there, if you wish."

Augustinia thanked me and the two removed their coats, draping them over the chair backs, and laid their umbrellas across the table. When they'd taken their chairs, I sat.

They were definitely visiting from the time of King Edward. Their hats and dresses were straight out of a costume rental shop. I wondered if there was some festival going on that had escaped my attention.

Augustinia smiled. "So what exactly is a hard asset lender?"

Both women were stunningly beautiful. Not at all what I was used to seeing in lesbian couples. And I just about dropped the conversational ball by staring at them. They, though, said nothing. Just sat with hands folded on the table and smiles on their faces and in their eyes. They knew they were beautiful and were amused by my reaction.

I cleared my throat. "Well, a hard asset lender is one who lends money and takes a hard asset as collateral against the loan. The loans are usually no longer than a year."

The two women looked at each other and then turned their attention back to me. Hester spoke.

"We run Betsy's Best Books. It's a block over on Second Street. We've been open for eight months. We moved here from New Orleans ten months ago."

"Your accents tell me you aren't originally from New Orleans."

Augustinia, her smile radiant, said, "Very perceptive of you, Mr. Thurgood. We are originally from southern Illinois."

"What kind of bookstore do you run?"

Hester answered. "General trade, with a strong emphasis on romance. Romance readers are voracious and they keep the lights on."

"Makes sense to stock what's popular."

"It's the eighty percent that gives us eighty percent of our income from the shop."

"Interesting. Usually it's the twenty percent that yields eighty percent of the income."

Augustinia nodded. "Usually. Such, though, is the nature of romance."

"At least in books," Hester added.

"Sometimes in real life," I said.

Augustinia took Hester's hand in hers and raised it to her lips and kissed it. "Yes, sometimes in real life as well."

It seemed to me Ms. Red was teasing me. But to not get side-tracked, I guided the conversation back to business.

"What exactly is it you need money for?"

Augustinia let go of Hester's hand, and folded hers primly in front of her on the table. "An estate is being sold off. The man was a book and pipe collector. We informed the tobacco shop couple about the pipes. We want the books and can buy the entire collection for twelve thousand nine hundred and fifty-seven dollars. The shipping will add another three hundred and thirty dollars. The value of the books at retail is approximately forty to fifty thousand dollars. We'd like a loan of thirteen thousand five hundred dollars."

"That sounds like a very good deal for you. But unless the books are romance novels, I don't think you'll be able to pay me back within a year. Unless I'm missing something here."

"That is a reasonable assumption," Augustinia said. "But summer is coming and the influx of tourists should result in a considerable increase in our sales revenue."

"And if worse comes to worse," Hester said, "we can borrow against the principal of our inheritance."

"Although we'd prefer not to, as that would reduce our living until the amount was repaid."

I considered what they said. Apparently, they lived off of the proceeds of an inheritance. Getting a closeup view of their dress, the fabric and tailoring told me I was wrong thinking they were costume shop goods. The clothes had to be custom made. The tailoring was just too fine. And the fabric was top notch. Therefore, their "living" must be sizable.

"So tell me this, Ms. Faber and Ms. Galt, just what exactly is your income?"

Once again, they turned their heads, looked at each other, and then turned back to face me. Something spooky in all of that, and quite honestly, I felt the proverbial chill in my spine.

Augustinia spoke. "Our great-great-grandfather Faber earned a substantial sum of money in railroads in the late eighteen hundreds. By today's standard, if taken as an amount relative to the total economic output of the economy, he was worth eighty-eight billion dollars.

"Grandfather Faber believed in generational wealth and encouraged his children and grandchildren to add to the family fortune. Our share of the family trust gives us a living of a quarter of a million dollars a year. We also own rental properties that give us an additional one hundred thousand a year."

"You are two exceedingly well-off women. Why come to me for a loan? You could easily get what you need from a bank. And at less interest than I will charge you."

"Grandfather Faber lost nearly half of his wealth in the panic of eighteen ninety-three. He did not trust banks after that. And neither do we."

"I see. But can't you float the money you need yourselves?"

"We need to act quickly, and we don't have that much cash available. At present."

"If I loan you the money, what do you have to put up as collateral?"

They did the head turn and look at each other thing again. When their eyes were back on me, Hester said, "Our current inventory at the bookstore is worth sixty-two thousand dollars. Will you accept that as collateral?"

"Not sure I want to get into the bookstore business. You've nothing else?"

"Nothing we're willing to risk losing," Augustinia said.

"Very well. The terms are fifteen percent interest each month on the outstanding principal, payable on the last business day of the month. The loan principal is to be paid in full by a year from now. A default on an interest payment or the principal results in my taking possession of the collateral."

"Monthly payment?" Augustinia asked.

"No set amount. Whatever you wish to pay, but it has to be at least a dollar."

"Your terms are acceptable to us," Augustinia said, then asked, "Is there something we sign?"

"Yes. Let me draw up the form."

I opened my iPad and, while completing the contract, asked, "You appear to have a lot of money. I'm still puzzled why you'd risk your inventory for such a small amount of cash."

They did the head maneuver again before Hester answered.

"We had another reason for doing business with you. We heard about you and we had to see for ourselves whether or not you would do."

"What do you mean by that?"

"All in due time, Mr. Thurgood," Augustinia said. "All in due time."

# 11

## FRIDAY, JANUARY 10, 8:21 PM

I'M NOT one for parties, to be honest, but to show Reece we were not the kind of people to hold grudges for little things like being falsely arrested, we attended the late holiday party he and Hetta were throwing for friends.

Ember was slowly working the living room. At the moment, she was talking with Brandon Turner, Joyce Blackstone, Sheriff Blanton, and Deputy Detective Maddy Dawson.

It was well known in town that Brandon and Reece were not the best of friends. In fact, I doubt one could even call them frenemies. So I was surprised to see him at Reece's party.

I was hanging out with the wall in the living room of the Sovern home, letting my eyes take in everyone there. More fun to watch people than to interact with them.

Because the living room wasn't overly large, guests were also in the kitchen, where the food and drink were, and in the family room.

I felt a presence next to me, followed by a voice sounding in my ear.

"You see that, don't you?"

The voice belonged to Graham Huston.

"You referring to Brandon being here in the Sovern living room?"

"Yep. I never thought I'd ever see the day when Turner would step foot in Reece's home."

"It is something that he was not only invited but that he accepted."

"If rumors are to be believed, it was Hetta who asked Joyce."

"Ah, the women trying to mend fences."

"If rumors are to be believed."

"Right. If they're to be believed. Did Reece or Hetta invite you?"

"No. I'm crashing this party."

"Must be a slow news day."

"I have Rob Carter at the college football game and Thomas Hedrick over at the high school game."

"Where's Monika?"

"She's pursuing something for her gossip column."

"So, why are you here?"

"With most of the Magnolia Bluff and Burnet County constabulary at Reece's party, I figure if anything is going to happen on the major or even minor crime scene, I'll be where the action is."

"Makes sense. Only don't let Reece see you."

"I'm not afraid of Reece. I'll simply promise to do a puff piece about him in the paper and all will be well."

I chuckled and made a comment about flattery getting him everywhere, when he said, "And look at that, here he comes now."

Our intrepid police investigator joined us, his chocolate Lab, Pickett, at his side.

"Don't stand there holding up the wall, Thurgood. Go on into the kitchen and get yourself some grub. Then mingle with the folks here or in the family room." He eyed Graham. "Slow news day, Huston?"

"Just figured I'd grab some eats and hang out with the local constabulary."

"Follow me, then, and get your eats."

Reece took off towards a doorway at the other end of the living room.

"Let's go, Harry, and get us some grub. Besides, rumor has it Reece's daughter is here visiting. She's not in the living room. Might be in the kitchen."

"I'm married."

"I'm not. And supposedly she's some kind of internet journalist. In L.A."

I shook my head, chuckled, and followed Graham, who was elbowing his way past people to catch up with Reece.

There were indeed eats in the kitchen. Sandwiches, potato salad, coleslaw, chips, homemade Christmas cookies, and several appetizers. The drinks included mulled cider, red and white wine, whiskey, brandy, vodka, a variety of mixers, sparkling water, coffee, and tea.

Reece told us to help ourselves and left.

I said hello to Hetta, Reece's wife, who, in turn, introduced me to their daughter, Annie Kate.

Graham was already engaged in conversation with her while he ate potato chips and coleslaw.

I said to Hetta, "Glad to see you and Joyce got Brandon to come."

"Reece wasn't happy, but grudgingly agreed maybe they could bury the hatchet." She paused, then began, "I just want to say I'm sorry—"

My upraised hand stopped her. "You have nothing to be sorry for. What's past is past. Today's today. And who knows what tomorrow will bring, but hopefully something better than today."

"You are a kind man, Mr. Thurgood."

"Harry."

"Okay, Harry. Thank you for that. Reece is—"

I cut her off. "He's honest and has a good heart."

"Yes, he is and I think so, too."

"This food looks good and I'm going to overindulge."

Hetta laughed. "Enjoy." She turned her attention to a youngish man I didn't know.

I filled my plate with a ham and cheese sandwich, potato salad, and coleslaw. After looking over the beverage offerings, I mixed myself a brandy and soda.

Then juggling glass and plate, I made my way to the family room to see who was there.

I found several of Magnolia Bluff's finest, along with a couple of Burnet County's finest, and two young men I didn't recognize.

Standing with the two young men and Captain Briggs was MBPD patrol officer Hans Winkler. He waved and called out, "Howdy Mr. Thurgood."

I stepped over to where he was standing and said hello.

He said, "I believe you've met Captain Briggs."

"I have. Happy new year, Captain."

Briggs, having just taken a bit of a sandwich, nodded his head.

Hans continued. "These two are Reece's boys. John, who is a patrol officer in the Fort Worth police department, and Ben, who works for a security firm in Houston."

With my hands full, I simply said hello and wished them a happy new year.

Hans informed the young men that I was a member of the MBPD Citizen Advisory Board.

Captain Briggs, having swallowed his bite of sandwich, said, "And that's as much involvement as a citizen should have. Don't you agree, Mr. Thurgood?"

"Not sure what you mean, Davis. Are you saying you don't want citizens to call in emergencies or suspicious activity?"

I watched Hans turn away and choke back his laugh.

"Not at all," Briggs said. "That's what *they* should do and leave the investigating to the professionals."

I was nonplussed by his comment and said, "I agree. As long as the professionals are up to the task. After all, there are auto mechanics and then there are auto mechanics. For example."

Briggs's eyes narrowed. Then he relaxed and a smile spread across his face. "That's very true. It pays to understand enough about your car so that you can select the best professional to do the job. I'm willing to wager you don't take that fancy foreign car of yours to a backyard tinkerer."

I liked how he got "professional" in there and then put it in juxtaposition with tinkerer. He was definitely death on amateurs. So I responded in kind. "No, I don't. But if I found a backyard mechanic who was better than a professional, I'd take my car to him. After all, I want the best work done by the best person who can do it. It's the work that counts. Not if the person is a pro or an amateur."

Briggs set his plate and glass down on an end table. He turned to Reece's boys. "Pleased to meet you. Duty calls, though, and I need to get back to the station."

When he was gone, Hans said, "It seems the captain doesn't like you, Harry."

"It does indeed. I can't imagine why."

"Word has it that he's pretty perturbed at how lax we are with allowing civilians to get involved in official investigations. He calls it interference."

"If he can do a better job, more power to him. Quite honestly, I'd *rather* have the professionals do what they were hired to do. After all, it is what we pay you guys for."

"I do my best."

"I know you do, Hans. You're a candle shining in the dark."

## 12

### FRIDAY, JANUARY 10, 8:59 PM

HAVING FINISHED EATING my food while talking with Reece's boys, I swallowed my drink and deposited the plate in the kitchen on my way to find Ember. But not before refilling my glass.

She was in the living room talking to MBPD officers Helen Beauregard and Kristine Combs. I stood beside my sweetie and slipped my arm around her waist.

Kristine said, "We were just telling Ember that Captain Briggs is going to be a real hard ass to work for."

I took a sip of my drink and let my shoulders rise and fall. "He can say whatever he wants. However, every organization has a culture. It takes a long time to change a culture. In addition, there's a community and what it will tolerate or not. So, I wouldn't be too worried if I were you."

"I'm not. I think the first ones who will feel his thumb are Reece and GJ."

Helen chimed in. "And GJ will follow what Briggs says, as if she was goose-stepping in formation."

Then, her voice barely audible, Kristine said, "I wonder when she's going to start hitting on him?"

The two women laughed heartily. I shook my head and

explained to Ember why they were laughing. She was about to say something when Graham and Annie Kate joined us.

Helen said, "Uh-oh. Now the press is here. We'll have to watch what we say."

Ember poked Graham in the ribs. "Nothing's sacred with this guy around."

"I can't believe you're saying that, Rev, after all I did to make you look really good."

The women, except for Annie Kate, who had a puzzle expression on her face, groaned.

I shook my head and explained to Annie Kate that my coffee shop was called the Really Good by the locals and was the focal point of a never ending stream of puns.

Graham, a grin on his face, continued on. "I'm trying to talk Annie here into writing for the *Chronicle* and maybe even help put us online."

I said to Reece's daughter, "You'd move from L.A.?"

She chuckled. "We're in negotiations, you might say. Nothing definite."

Suddenly Reece and Georgia Jean made a beeline for the front door. They were followed by Hans Winkler and most of the other Magnolia Bluff police force at the party, along with several of the deputies.

Helen and Kristine looked at each other, said, "men" in unison, excused themselves, and headed for the entryway and front door.

Graham was right behind them. "C'mon," he said over his shoulder. "Hot news, and you're now on my payroll as reporters."

---

Cop cars were everywhere and Kristine was stringing up crime scene tape to cordon off the area around the high school boating dock.

Graham was wandering around, trying to find someone who'd talk to him. Annie Kate took a drone out of the trunk of her rental car and launched it. Briggs was going to love that.

"I have a feeling we have another murder on our hands," Ember said.

"Not *our* hands," I corrected.

Annie Kate called out, "There's a body floating off the end of the dock."

A shot rang out, Annie Kate said, "Damn," and a voice bellowed, "Who's drone was that?"

"Incredible," I muttered.

"What is?" Ember asked.

"That Briggs shot down Annie Kate's drone."

Annie Kate must've heard us. With her fists clenched, she marched across the parking lot, ducked under the crime scene tape, and got right into Briggs's face.

"You owe me five hundred dollars for that drone," she shouted.

Briggs stepped back, whipped out his handcuffs, and said, "You're under arrest for interfering in a police investigation."

"I'm a journalist making a live report on a possible murder."

"Turn around and put your hands behind your back."

"Do you know who I am? I'm Reece—"

"I don't care if you're the Virgin Mary herself. Now turn around."

"I will not, you arrogant pig!"

Briggs took a step towards her, and Annie Kate took off running.

I was surprised at how fast the captain could move, as he's a pretty big guy.

He wrapped her up in a dozen steps like a safety stopping the wide receiver from making a touchdown, and had her face down on the ground, knee in her back, and then hands cuffed behind her back.

Briggs yanked her to her feet, none too gentle, hauled her

over to his car, and stuffed her into the back seat, and closed the door. I noticed he hadn't bothered to protect her head putting her in the car.

"Attention!" he bellowed. "Anyone here who is not law enforcement has one minute to leave or you will be arrested." He looked at his watch. "The minute starts now."

"Well, Mister," Ember began, "I think that's our cue to go home."

"Well, Rev, I think you're right. Do you see Graham anywhere?"

"No, I don't."

"He's resourceful, and he doesn't live far from here. He should be okay."

"If he heeds the captain's warning."

"There is that."

Walking to the car, Ember said, "I hope Reece can talk his boss into releasing his daughter. I thought law enforcement stuck together. You know, all for one and one for all."

"Briggs is trying to prove a point. But I don't see how arresting the daughter of his chief investigator is a good motivational move."

"Doesn't make sense to me."

"I did arrange for a little surprise to be waiting for him at the station."

"A surprise for Briggs?"

"Yep. While he was tackling Annie Kate, I texted Stanton. He should be waiting for them when they arrive."

"Oh, that's wicked, Mister."

"Perhaps. I know Stanton will appreciate a late-night snack, so to speak."

Ember giggled. "He's a piranha, that's for sure. The captain won't know what hit him."

# 13

## FRIDAY, JANUARY 10, 11:21 PM

Reece Sovern was not a happy camper. Not after he'd learned that his superior officer had arrested his daughter.

He was driving the five-minute drive to the station from the high school. GJ was with him and he could sense she was really up.

"Boy, did you see Briggs arrest those journalists? Man, he's awesome. He'll bring some professionalism to the department."

"We haven't been professional?" Reece kept to himself the fact that one of those journalists was his own daughter.

"I don't mean to speak badly about the chief, but he doesn't keep good boundaries."

"What do you mean?"

"He's too friendly with that Bliss Jager, and definitely too friendly with Caroline McCluskey."

Reece thought he picked up a hint of jealousy there.

She went on. "And then there's Thurgood and the Reverend. What's up with that?"

Reece made a deprecating sound, and she continued, "And then there's that arrogant asshole, Turner. Always trying to make you look bad. And Tommy's all, 'Oh, Brandon, help us hayseeds out. We're too stupid to catch a criminal.' What the hell is up with that? The chief is supposed to have our back's."

Reece pulled into the station parking lot and parked in his spot. After shutting the engine off, he reached over and put his hand on GJ's arm. "It's okay."

"I mean, you're a good cop, Sarge. Dedicated. And honest. *Honest*. Can we say that about Turner?"

"Yes, we can." Realizing he'd left his hand a bit too long on GJ's arm, he gave her a pat and put his hand on the steering wheel.

"We can? For sure?"

"Yes. He was a good cop who got framed."

"If you say so."

"I do. And now he's retired. But we cops never retire. It's in our blood to serve and protect."

"You're right there."

"So he's just doing what we'd probably do ourselves: stick our noses in where they don't belong."

"I guess."

"And now I have to see Briggs and try to talk him out of booking my daughter."

"Wait... What?"

"She was one of the journalists."

"Oh, God. Oh, Sarge, I'm so sorry. I—"

"Don't worry about it. Changing the subject, you going to the defensive pistol meet tomorrow?"

"I was planning on it, but with another murder and this one on our turf..."

"Let's go. My boys, John and Ben are going. If something big happens, they can call me."

"Okay, Sarge. It'll be fun. Maybe it will be my day to finally beat you."

Reece smiled. "Good luck with that."

He opened his car door, GJ followed suit, and they exited the vehicle.

"Anything I can do to help? You know, with Briggs?"

"Yeah, there is. Come with me and make sure I don't punch his lights out."

# 14

## SATURDAY, JANUARY 11, 5:48 AM

THE SKY WAS DARK. The drizzle had started two hours ago and showed no signs of letting up.

Elder Smythe and John Paul had just finished dropping off the morning delivery. I'd come in early to take care of it because Miguel planned on roasting coffee beans before we opened.

"Is that it?" I asked.

Elder Smythe said, "Six dozen eggs. Fifteen pounds of chicken. Four cabbages. Three pounds of kale. And three pounds of mushrooms. That's it."

He handed me the receipt. I paid him in cash and gave him two pounds of city roast Kenya AA coffee beans as a tip.

"Appreciate the coffee, Mr. Thurgood. May God bless you."

"He has abundantly."

Sometimes it's just better to tell people what they want to hear. Most days, I don't believe in a god as imagined by Christians, which, of course, leads to some interesting discussions with Em. Then again, she has beliefs that would make even liberal Christians scream heretic.

John Paul and the elder got in the truck. We waved to each other, and they drove off.

I returned to the kitchen, glad to be out of the drizzle. After shucking my raincoat, I put the delivery items away, and placed six loaves of tomato basil bread in the oven to bake.

Noonan, of Bluff Bakery, was tapping the glass of the front door. I briskly walked to the door, unlocked it, and relieved him of the boxes of baked goods he had in his hands.

We bake a lot of our own goodies, well, Miguel does, but sometimes Noonan and his crew just do it better.

I was placing the doughnuts, pastries, and pie on display when I heard more tapping on the glass of the front door. The person trying to get my attention this time was Graham Huston. I unlocked the door and let him in.

"Morning Graham. Come on in out of the liquid sunshine."

"Thanks, Harry. May I have a cup of coffee?"

"Sure thing. Hungry?"

"The stomach could use a fill."

"Anything in particular?"

"Would French toast be too much of a bother?"

"For you? Nah. Follow me to the kitchen."

"Thanks for the services of your legal beagle."

"Don't mention it."

"That Briggs is something else. Reece was pissed, got into a shouting match with him, and GJ had to intervene."

"Wish I could have been the proverbial fly on the wall."

"You could hear them all over the station."

"Then Briggs started a go-to with Stanton and Stanton calmly shut him down by telling him he was filing a harassment suit against him, Tommy, the department, and the city."

I lifted my head and let loose a roar of laughter. "Wish I could have seen *that*."

"So Briggs let Annie and me go and didn't end up charging us with anything. She said she's going to pursue the harassment suit."

"Huh. Looks as though our new captain has bitten off more than he can chew. You don't want to pursue a harassment suit?"

"Don't need to. I have a newspaper going out to four thousand households with big, bold headlines. Could I have some sausage with the French toast?"

# 15

## SATURDAY, JANUARY 11, 8:37 AM

Reece pushed open the door of the Really Good and entered the shop.

The drizzle had managed to penetrate his raincoat enough to make his suit damp. Thank goodness he'd covered his old trilby with the plastic hat wrap. Otherwise it would have been a sodden mess.

He walked over to Harry's table where the man himself sat.

"Slow coffee day?" Reece said, hooking his thumb towards the empty tables.

"The weather. When it rains, it will be one of two extremes with customers: empty or mobbed."

Reece pulled out a chair and sat.

"Coffee? Something to eat?" Harry asked.

"Yeah. That sounds good. You have biscuits and gravy on that fancy New York menu?"

Harry chuckled. "I learned real fast to have biscuits and gravy."

Reece watched him signal to Estrelita for the coffee and then he told her B and G.

"Your breakfast will be here in a jiffy."

"Thanks, Harry." He cleared his throat. "And I want to thank you for sending Lauderbach to help my daughter."

"My pleasure. Freedom of the press and all."

"Yeah, right."

"I heard you and your boss had a bit of a set to."

"Man, word gets around fast."

"Graham was here earlier."

"Okay. That explains it. Yeah, it wasn't pretty. I think Briggs finally saw daylight when Lauderbach told him he would be filing a harassment suit."

"Two months on the job and he gets hit with a lawsuit. That can't be good."

"No. Not really. Say, uh, Harry, Lauderbach ain't cheap. And I do appreciate what you did, and so fast, but I really can't—"

Estrelita set a mug of coffee and a plate of biscuits and gravy before Reece. He told her thanks, and she left. He picked up his fork, and put it back down.

"As I was saying, I—"

He watched Harry wave it away. "On me," he said.

"Look, I understand you have money, but no one has unlimited money."

"True that. Don't worry about your daughter. I got it covered and Stanton isn't asking for my firstborn. So we're good. Okay?"

Reece picked up his fork. "If you say so. Thanks." He conveyed biscuit and gravy to his mouth and nodded his satisfaction.

"So we had another murder?" Harry asked.

Reece nodded. "This is on the QT. Understand?"

"Sure."

"This is number seven. The first one in our jurisdiction. The other bodies have been found around the county. Which means Buck and his crew have been investigating those."

"Are all of them by the same person?"

"Looks that way. All the bodies have been exsanguinated, and the livers removed. Two bodies apparently looked like they'd been butchered for meat. Otherwise, all seven are the same."

"That's pretty gruesome. So why are you telling me this?"

"You're a pretty thoughtful investigator. I might want to talk to you about the case. Get some insight. You know?"

"Okay. Always glad to help, although I'm not a cop."

"I know. But you are a natural at this investigating stuff. So I might run some things by you. Get your take on different scenarios."

"If you need to think out loud, I'm here."

"Thanks. And don't tell Huston. We want this out of the paper. Out of the limelight. No need to be scaring folks."

"Okay."

Reece put biscuit and gravy in his mouth and studied the coffee shop owner's face and body language while he chewed.

*He sure looks cool as a cucumber. Completely in control. I wonder what his story is?*

He swallowed food, took a sip of coffee, and asked, "How are mom and the twins doing?"

Harry smiled. "Well, Em's bored. Wants to go back to work. Says she has nothing to do, now that we have Clara, our nanny, and Jearlene taking care of things."

Reece grunted. "I sure as hell would like time to do a whole lot of nothing."

"Knowing you, I'd give you a week, two at the most, before you'd be itching to do something."

Reece nodded. "Yeah, you're probably right." He finished his breakfast, drank up the coffee, and stood. "Best get back at it."

"Thanks for stopping by. Hope you enjoyed the biscuits and gravy."

"I did. They were…" Reece smiled. "Really good."

"Knew that was coming. Have a good day, Sarge."

"You too."

Reece paid Jack for the food. Insisting, even after Harry had said it was on the house.

"Don't need charity," he told Jack Bonhoffer. "At least not yet."

Out on the sidewalk, he repositioned his glasses, removed the cellophane from an emerald green corona, and sank his teeth into it.

*Now to see who our victim is and what she was doing in our town.*

## 16

### SATURDAY, JANUARY 11, 9:34 AM

THE TABLE WAS rectangular and long. Long enough to seat twenty-eight people comfortably.

At one end of the table sat Gunter Fight. He was dressed in brown cotton slacks and a blue, green, and black plaid long sleeve shirt.

To his right sat his wife, Mary Lou, and to his left sat his adopted daughter, Oralene. Mary Lou always let Gunter sit at the head of the table. She felt it was good for his ego.

The Queen of the Crimson Hats was wearing a deep burgundy dress with a subtle dark blue and black paisley pattern.

Oralene had put on a dark blue pleated skirt, a winter white blouse, and a forest green cardigan sweater. She'd never had such fine clothes as what were now in her possession. All thanks to Mother Fight.

On the table was a pitcher of orange juice; a pot of coffee; platters of ham, bacon, and scrambled eggs; a plate of buttered toast; bowls of blueberry, cherry, peach, and strawberry jam; and a bowl of grits. An ordinary breakfast for the Fight household.

Oralene drank orange juice and ate a slice of toast with peach jam. When the toast was gone, she said, "Tomorrow's the day, Mother. You are returning home."

Mary Lou set down her fork. "To my home church, yes. Rumor has it that Miss Cole may cut short her maternity leave. I wish to hear Reverend Humphrey speak before the strumpet once again usurps the pulpit."

"The look on her face when she sees you. I can't wait to see it."

Gunter ate ham and then turned a page in the *Austin American* newspaper. "You women are making a lot of nonsense over nothing, if you ask me."

Mary Lou picked up her fork, said, "No one did," and conveyed the egg it contained to her mouth.

Gunter didn't look at her. Eyes on the paper, a piece of ham at the ready on his fork, he continued, "Just go to the damn church. All this fussing about nothing. That woman won't be there forever. I don't understand why you haven't told the bishop to move her already."

The ham disappeared into his mouth, and he turned a page.

"You take care of the bank and I'll take care of Saint Luke's."

Gunter grunted and speared another piece of ham.

Mary Lou addressed Oralene. "Never let a man, even if he is your husband, control you. We women have always run the world. Behind every successful man is a woman. Make sure, my dear, *you* are that woman."

"Yes, Mother."

"Reverend Humphrey will be our guest tomorrow for dinner. He is not married. Perhaps he will make a favorable impression on you."

"You want me to marry *him*?"

"Why not? His family has money and is well connected, which means they have influence. And influence is power. I believe an uncle is a senator. A cousin is a congressman. Another uncle is a bishop. And someone else is an ambassador to some important country. You could do a lot worse than marrying Reverend Humphrey, and scarcely better."

"I've heard he's a homosexual."

"And what difference does that make? If he wants to get ahead, he will keep all that in the closet. Those people are in the open now, but they are still considered not like us. If they want to get ahead, they will pretend they are normal."

"But what about children?"

"If you want them, have them. No one is stopping you. You're a clever woman. You'll figure it out."

"Yes, Mother, I am. I will figure it out. I will figure it all out."

## 17

### SATURDAY, JANUARY 11, 9:35 AM

TIPPER DUVALL, the Lay Leader at Saint Luke's United Methodist Church, sat in the morning room drinking coffee and smoking Turkish cigarettes in a long cigarette holder.

She thought of tomorrow morning and of Mary Lou Fight's return to her church, and it made Tipper nervous. No one knew she was a secret member of the Crimson Hat Society and Mary Lou had impressed on her that all must go well.

Tipper, however, had no idea what she could actually do to make sure all went well.

She had notified the Reverend Adelbert Humphrey that Mrs. Fight would be returning to the church and that she would appreciate a special pastoral welcome. The Reverend Humphrey had assured Tipper that a welcome for such an august person as Mrs. Fight would indeed be given.

While Tipper didn't like the simpering cleric, she agreed with her Queen that Reverend Humphrey was easily controlled. He wasn't a loose cannon. Unlike Reverend Cole, who was unpredictable, had loose morals, and took up with questionable men.

Tipper took a deep drag on her cigarette, inhaled, held the smoke, and then exhaled a long plume towards the ceiling.

*Of course, we're not aware if Bertie takes up with questionable men or not. Although, I assume Mary Lou knows if he does or doesn't. Not that it matters since the anti-gay party left the denomination.*

She drank coffee.

*Then again, there are plenty at Saint Luke's who are anti-gay.*

She'd heard herself called on more than one occasion a fag hag just for talking to Humphrey. Nevertheless, she was confident should Ember Cole depart, the congregation would welcome the Reverend Humphrey, Uranian or not. He got on so well with all of the old women.

Tipper tapped ash into the ashtray. With Mary Lou returning, the only question was how soon would Ember Cole be vacating her office.

---

The bell over the door rang and I watch Monika Crow bounce into the Really Good, a newspaper tucked under one arm, and a blue denim purse hanging from the shoulder of the other.

She was wearing light blue slacks, a burgundy blouse with white polka dots, and a light green scarf around her neck.

Crossing the floor to my table, she held out the paper. "You didn't come in to get this earlier, so I thought I'd drop it off. Free of charge. Tips accepted, of course."

I laughed at that. "You already get free coffee." I took the paper from her.

"I do at that. Okay, we're good."

"Say, can you tell me anything about the murder victim?"

"Are you playing super sleuth again?"

"No, just curious. With Briggs arresting your boss, I just wanted to know if we knew anything about the person."

"All I know is that Tommy and Buck are keeping this very hush-hush."

"Seems odd, doesn't it?"

"The official line is that they don't want people to panic.

They're working with the Rangers. And all the victims are not from here. So we locals don't have to worry."

"And that's it?"

"That's all I know. Why? Do you know something else?"

"Nope. Just curious."

"Okay. Gotta run. Tootles." She wiggled her fingers at me and bounced back out the door.

I took a bite of my doughnut. *We don't have to worry until one of our own gets exsanguinated and eviscerated.*

# 18

## SATURDAY, JANUARY 11, 12:08 PM

EMBER HELD one twin in each arm. They were sleeping contentedly, their little bellies full of milk. They were beautiful babies. Ruddy, with bright blue eyes.

Monette had a patch of dark hair on her head, but Maximillian was a baldy. Clara had told mom that was normal.

"Would you like me to take the little ones so you can get lunch, ma'am?"

"Not yet, Clara. I want to hold these two precious gifts a little while longer."

"I don't blame you, ma'am. You can always eat. But they are this precious for such a short period of time."

"But aren't children always precious?"

"Of course, ma'am. But not as these two are now. They grow and change. Gradually becoming independent persons. Adults. Precious, but a vastly different precious from what they are at this moment."

"Yes. I understand."

"Perhaps Mr. Thurgood should hire a housekeeper and cook for the weekends. To fill in for Mrs. Reston. Very nice of him to give her the weekends off."

"She has young children of her own and needs to spend time with them."

"You're very considerate of her."

"Jerri hasn't had the easiest life. Hopefully, we've helped change that."

"I'm sure you have, ma'am. She's very grateful for the salary Mr. Thurgood pays her."

"He's a generous man."

"That he is. More than generous. Touch wood he has a long and healthy life."

"Amen, Clara. Amen."

"And you as well, ma'am. A man needs a good woman by his side."

"Thank you."

The doorbell rang.

"I'll get it, ma'am."

"Thanks, Clara."

In a moment, the nanny returned. "The Reverend Mister Humphrey wishes to know if you are receiving. His words, ma'am."

"I do think he was born in the wrong century. I'll see him. Here, why don't you take the twins and I'll get the door."

"Very good, ma'am."

Ember handed the babies to Clara, who took them upstairs to the nursery, while she went to the door.

She couldn't believe her eyes. The Reverend Adelbert Humphrey the fourth was wearing some manner of odd looking suit.

The cutaway black coat had a single button in the middle which the Reverend Humphrey had left unbuttoned. Ember supposed it was so he could show off the beautiful camel hair vest, which was fully buttoned. The trousers were dark gray, with even darker gray pinstripes. The shirt was white and had a wing collar. Around his neck was a lavender satin puff tie. The only thing identifying him as a clergyman, not that most people would understand the symbolism, was the old Anglican shovel hat he was wearing.

Ember invited him in. He removed his hat, bowed, and said, "Good afternoon, Reverend Cole."

She wished him a good afternoon as well and asked him to follow her to the living room.

"You have a lovely home. It certainly is a marvelous display of wealth and power."

Ember indicated a chair in which he could sit and she sat in one opposite. She noticed he sat very straight, with his knees together, hat in his lap, and hands folded in front of him.

*He is truly strange,* she said to herself. To him she said, "This home was built by an old rail baron. They were into such displays in the eighteen hundreds."

"So they were. But I understand that your husband has the means to maintain the tradition."

Ember's eyes narrowed. "The home was for sale. Had been for some time and Harry bought it at a good price. A bargain, considering."

"Oh, I'm sure. I'm sure."

"So how may I help you, Mister Humphrey? Or are you here on a social call?" Ember realized her voice was more brusque than was necessary.

"Well!" There was a look of surprise on his face. He recovered quickly, however. "No, I'm not on a social call, Ms. Cole. I'm here on church business. You see, Mrs. Fight returns to Saint Luke's tomorrow and the worship committee thought it best if one of their members did the reading from the Gospel. After all, we wouldn't want to upset one of our largest donors now, would we?"

"I see." Ember paused, then said, "I will have you know, Mr. Thurgood gave more to Saint Luke's last year than the Fights ever did. So I would like you to explain to me the logic of thumbing your nose at the wife of the man who has given more to Saint Luke's in one year than most have given in their lifetimes. Explain that to me, Mr. Humphrey."

"Well, uh, you see—"

"Never mind. You can't explain it because there is no logical explanation. It's the Fight mystique. And you are enamored by it."

Ember stood. "Do what you need to do. I shall notify the bishop that I am ending my maternity leave early. Monday morning I will be returning to God's church to do my duty as His servant. I do believe our conversation is over."

"Well!" Humphrey stood and followed Ember to the door.

He bowed, wished her a good day, and left.

She watched him get in his car and closed the door when he drove off.

"What a simpering idiot," she said under her breath.

After a moment, she confessed, "I'm sorry Lord. That was mean of me. But, I'm so tired of the disrespect." She took a deep breath. "Yes, I'm very much aware that you suffered more and my trials are nothing compared to yours. But I'm not You. I'm human. I'm frail compared to You." Then she smiled. "Yes, I remember. You will not test me beyond what I can handle. So I guess I can handle Bertie and Mary Lou."

She headed back to the family room, and on the way decided that tomorrow would be a good day to do some open air preaching at the college.

## 19

### SATURDAY, JANUARY 11, 2:19 PM

CAPTAIN BRIGGS READ AGAIN the printout of the email the Medical Examiner had sent him.

It was all straightforward. An as yet unidentified white female found floating off the high school boating dock. She was naked and had been in the water for several days. Probably killed around the time of the full moon. Her system contained the drug Phrancinol, she'd been exsanguinated, and finally she'd had her liver removed.

"The same MO as the six victims Blanton's people are investigating," Briggs muttered.

He picked up the stack of files, copies of the ones the sheriff's CI people had sent over, and paged through them.

The victims were four women and three men. None of them local. Each had been killed around the time of the full moon.

*Where do we begin? Is there some manner of Satanic cult around here? And why were these people in the county in the first place?*

He pushed the files aside.

*Was our victim staying here in town, or somewhere else in the county? Hopefully, the artist sketch we've posted around town will spark someone's memory.*

He picked up a pencil and toyed with it, while leaning back in his chair. His mind taking a stroll through the data.

After nearly a minute, he sat up and tossed the pencil onto his desk.

"Sovern should be here busting his hump on this." His words stabbed the room. "But what's he doing instead of working? Spending valuable man-hours in a shooting competition. There needs to be some discipline around here. It's no wonder the chief is running all over town doing everything. No discipline. But then discipline should come down from the top."

He shook his head and forwarded the email with the ME's report to his sergeant investigator.

After a moment or two of staring at the computer screen and getting no answer to anything, Briggs stood and headed for the door.

*Maybe we need a new police chief.*

---

The bell over the door sounded, and I looked up to see who'd entered.

*Huh. What does Briggs want?*

The man's head turned to the right and then the left. When he spotted me, he marched to my table.

"You don't have a lot of business, do you?"

I deadpanned it. "It has picked up over the last year or two."

"Could've fooled me. Mind if I sit?"

I gestured towards a chair, and he sat.

"What can I do you for, Captain?"

"That's an odd way to say it."

"Not where I'm from."

"And where is that, exactly?"

I favored him with a smile. "Next question?"

"Ah, yes. The man of mystery. The man with the secret life.

The man with the hidden past. What are you hiding, Mr. Thurgood?"

"It's best if folks keep themselves to themselves. I like my privacy, and I intend to keep it that way."

"Why?"

"For me to know and not for you to find out."

Briggs made a deprecating sound, cleared his throat, and said, "Sergeant Sovern talk to you about the case?"

"You checking up on him? Making sure he doesn't talk to us civilians about police matters?"

"It's my job to make the Magnolia Bluff police department the best it can be, and that's what I'm doing, Mr. Thurgood."

"Well, Captain, as you can see, I don't have my consulting detective hat on. Feel better?"

"Not really. You see, you and your wife are big unknowns. I'm not overly concerned about the others the chief and my investigator talk to. But you and Mrs. Thurgood—"

"She's Reverend Cole. She's her own woman."

"I see. Well, let me tell you this: I don't like secrets. Hers is out of the bag, as I understand it, or at least some of it is out of the bag. But you? I figure with all the secrecy, you must be running or hiding from something. And that means you've probably had lots of contact with cops. And not good contact. Am I right?"

"Seeing as I don't have to talk to you, I think this part of our conversation has come to a brick wall."

"I see. Hm."

"While you're voicing your suspicions, would you like a coffee or something to eat?"

"Thanks, but I'm good."

"Mind if I ask you a question?"

"You can ask."

"Why did you apply for this job?"

He lifted his shoulders and let them drop. "Thought this would be a good place to retire. Winters aren't so brutal here."

"Makes sense. Brandon Turner said the same thing. Looks like it's working for him. Might work for you, too."

"I hope so."

"Look, Captain, I'm not sure how we got off on the wrong foot, but I hope we can get back on the right foot. Because if you're going to retire here and I'm going to retire here, we'll probably be seeing a lot of each other. It is, after all, a small town. And I'd rather have it that when we wave hello to each other, we mean it."

"As long as you don't think you're a cop and interfere in police business, we'll get along just fine."

"I don't and I won't. Since you're here now, I'm sure everything's going to be hunky-dory."

Brigg's eyes narrowed for a moment, but then he smiled and said, "Glad you think so, Mr. Thurgood." He stood. "And I hope I don't find out you're a crook on the run. Have a good day."

"You, too, Captain," but my words only reached his back because he was already on his way to the door.

When he was gone, I said to Jack and Estrelita, "He pays for his food and coffee. No freebies."

Jack chuckled. "Don't have to tell us twice. Pompous, sanctimonious prick. If he was a combat officer, someone would toss a grenade into his tent."

# 20

## SATURDAY, JANUARY 11, 6:02 PM

REECE SOVERN, his two sons, and Georgia Jean Riggins sat in the living room of the Sovern home. Hetta was putting the finishing touches on supper.

For at least the tenth time, GJ expressed her disbelief at how Reece had come from behind in the last round to beat her.

Ben, Reece's younger son, said, "It's Dad's military training. Gives him the edge."

"You weren't in combat, though, were you, Sarge?" GJ asked.

"Not in any of our official unofficial wars," Reece replied. "But I did find myself in a couple firefights in places no one's ever heard of and that's all I can say on the subject."

"That explains it," GJ said. "Nothing like combat to hone your skills."

"For the survivors," Reece added.

Hetta called them all to dinner and explained that Annie Kate was out with a friend.

"Male or female?" Reece asked.

"Amy Whiteman," Hetta answered. "Her dad had the gift shop, remember?"

Reece nodded.

"Kind of hard to forget that, Mom," John, the older son, said.

He turned to Reece and said, "You have an odd case on your hands, don't you, Dad?"

"Very. Not sure where to begin. How would you handle it up in Fort Worth?"

John laughed. "I'm a grunt. I just do what I'm told."

"Well, then, how would your boss handle it?" Reece countered.

"We'd do what you'd do: try to find out as much about the victim as we can and, in the process, hopefully figure out why the person was here."

Reece nodded. "Standard procedure."

"Yep," John said. "Just keep gathering information until something clicks."

"Hopefully we'll get a hit on her fingerprints soon," GJ said.

"There was no ID?" John asked.

Reece shook his head. "Not one bit. Not even a tattoo or birthmark."

"Yeah, that makes it rough," John said.

Reece's phone dinged. He conveyed a spoon of stew to his mouth.

Hetta said, "You might as well see who it is. And don't look so guilty. It's your job."

Reece put the spoon down, swallowed his food, took his phone out of his pocket, and looked at the text.

"Briggs," he said.

"What's he want?" GJ asked.

"Wants me to come in. Might have gotten our first break."

Reece texted back and said to his partner, "Eat up. Told him we'd be there in half an hour."

# 21

## SATURDAY, JANUARY 11, 7:56 PM

REECE, GJ, and Captain Briggs sat in the conference room at the station. The captain had made a fresh pot of coffee and had purchased a big bag of popcorn and a couple of bags of potato chips.

GJ poured herself a cup of coffee and filled a paper bowl with popcorn.

Reece would've preferred Hetta's bread pudding, but at least the boss had considered the troops. He had to give him credit for that.

*Enjoy the honeymoon for as long as it lasts,* he told himself.

Briggs cleared his throat. "The ME puts the time of death approximately two weeks ago, given the state of decomposition of the body. Which means she was possibly killed at the last full moon."

"And that means she is another victim of our Full Moon Killer," Reece said.

"Correct, Sergeant. As with the other victims, it looks as though she died from exsanguination. After that, her liver was removed."

"Have we IDed her yet?" GJ asked.

Briggs nodded. "We have. With help from the Rangers and

the FBI, we got a match on her fingerprints. Our victim is Kari Lynn Waskowski. Born in Chicago. Served three years in the army. Was honorably discharged. She was twenty-nine when she died."

"What was her MOS?" Reece asked.

Briggs gave him a blank look.

"What was her job in the army?" Reece clarified.

"I don't have that information, Sergeant. If you think it relevant, find out."

Reece made a note in his notebook. "Do we know why she was here?"

"No, we don't. Perhaps the answer is at her place of residence. Brookfield, Illinois. She was renting a room from an elderly couple. I've contacted the Brookfield police to get permission to search the room and for them to secure it in the meantime. Once we get the go ahead...," Briggs's eyes focused on Reece, "you or Georgia Jean will go to Illinois, conduct the search, and talk to everyone you can find connected to the victim. We have a start. Let's see where it leads us. And hopefully the artist sketches posted around town will jog someone's memory. You two know what to do."

Briggs stood and left the room.

Reece helped himself to a handful of potato chips.

"You going to Illinois, Sarge?"

"Cook County isn't Illinois. It's a third world hellhole unto itself. And no, I'm not. I don't like flying. Had enough of that with the Marines."

"You want me to go?"

"Sure. Why? Don't you want to?"

"I'd love to! I've never been outside Texas."

"I have, and I'll take Texas."

"I've never been on a plane, either."

"Ain't missing anything there. Personally, I'd take the train."

"You would?"

"Yep. See more of the country, and it's a lot more comfortable."

"I wish we could both go."

"You can handle it. Plus, you'll have those new experiences."

"I understand. It's just that we work better together, and I like watching you work. I learn so much from you."

"Well, uh, thanks. You're a great partner. We make a good team."

"I'm happy you feel that way, Sarge. We're good together."

*Whoa. I hope I'm misunderstanding the undercurrent I'm feeling here.* He cleared his throat. "Personally, we don't need to wait. Briggs said we know what to do. Go on home, pack a bag, and book yourself a flight to Chicago."

"Thanks, Sarge. Hopefully, Ms. Waskowski will have something in her room that will crack this case wide open."

---

Ember finished nursing Maximillian and held him in her arms. Harry was in the wingback next to hers holding Monette.

As if by magic, Clara appeared in order to take the little ones up to bed. Ember and Harry kissed the two babies and off they went to bed.

"Are you sure you won't come with me to the college tomorrow?"

"I'm sure. You have, what, half a dozen going already? You don't need me. Besides, I need to get the inventory list from those women. They didn't have it ready when I gave them the money."

"Rather trusting, weren't you?"

"As they say, I know where they live."

"And what's that supposed to mean?"

"It means I know where I can get that list of books."

"I see. Glad you clarified that."

"You aren't getting insecure on me, are you?"

"Nope. Just yanking your chain."

"Ah. Good. Back to your original question. You don't need me there at the college. I'll just be a fifth wheel. Besides, if there's time, I just might go to church and catch the Queen Bee's grand entrance. Might even record it."

"What on earth for?"

"Maybe Graham will want it."

"He might."

There was a brief lull, and then Ember asked, "You don't think we need to be concerned about this new murder, do you?"

"Not in the least. Especially with Briggs making sure no civilians are involved."

"I don't mean that. I mean, with the police coming after us."

"Why would they come after us?"

"It's just that we seem to have targets on our backs."

"Not anymore. Things have been pretty good between us and Reece."

"That's true. And I hope they stay that way."

"Probably they will."

"On a different note, with Mary Lou back at Saint Luke's, I've been debating if this might be a good time to move on."

"Say what?"

"I mean, things are just going to get worse and I'm tired of the hassle. I don't believe this hill is worth dying on anymore.

Ember saw Harry take a deep breath and slowly let it out.

"Well, Em, I'm not going to tell you how to run the church or whether you should stay or go. That's between you and your God."

"I know. But I do value your opinion. And I'm sure you have one."

"Oh, I have one all right."

"So, tell me."

"Okay. In my opinion, you should stay. A majority in the church support you. It's true that a fair number of the leadership positions are in the hands of the enemy. But they've been thwarted by the members pretty much every time they try something. The old guard is old. They are slowly dying off. Keep bringing in new bodies. Gradually fill the leadership positions. And voila, you'll have a new church. Just hang in there."

"It's been a big help since you've been attending the church council meetings."

"The opposition is dangerous, but they're not bright. Which, to my mind, ultimately reflects back on Mary Lou."

"Okay. I've put leaving in the trash can. No more leaving talk."

"Good. Do you need to work on your message for tomorrow?"

"No. I'm good to go."

"Great. You good to go on trying for number three?"

"Thought you'd never ask."

## 22

### SUNDAY, JANUARY 12, 8:12 AM

THERE WAS a knock on the door.

Reece said, "Come in."

The door opened and Officer Dick Schreiber poked his head in. "Hey, Sarge. Gotta guy out here who says he knows the woman in the artist sketch. Says it's his sister."

"Really? Send him in."

Schreiber left and in a minute brought back a tall, broad-shouldered man. His torso and arms looked like they belonged to a weight lifter.

What especially caught Reece's eye were the jet black spacers in his earlobes. The tiny diamonds in the centers glinted in the light.

Reece stood. "Have a seat."

"I know her," the man said. "She's my sister. Where is she?"

Reece pointed to the chair and sat. After a moment, the man did as well.

"She's dead. Isn't she?"

Reece nodded. "I'm afraid so. I'm deeply sorry for your loss. Truly."

"I knew it."

The man was holding it together, but just barely. Reece didn't say anything. He let the man process the information.

After a few moments, he asked, "Where is she? Her body, I mean?"

"In Austin for the autopsy. You mind telling me her name?"

"Kari Lynn Waskowski. She's, was, twenty-nine. Born in Chicago. Lives… Uh, lived in Brookfield."

"Was she in the military?"

"Yes. Army. Wanted to be like her big brother, but she didn't like it at all and left when her three years were up."

Reece nodded thoughtfully. "And you are?"

"Kyle Waskowski. Her big brother. She came here because some wacky cult group she got involved in asked her to come. When I didn't hear from her, I came to look for her."

"I'm truly sorry things have turned out this way. We'll take you to Austin for an official ID, although we verified most of what you just told us. Except the cult part. What can you tell me about that?"

"Nothing much. Didn't talk about the group. I think she thought I'd all find it too wacky, and from the little she said it was wacky."

"In what way?"

"Eternal life from eternal death and crap like that. The countesses promised an eternal life of meaning and purpose. And now she's dead."

"The countesses?"

"Yeah. Kari said she met these two women online in some chat room. They called themselves the countesses and promised you a life of meaning if you followed them. Eternal life from eternal death. And now she's dead all right."

Reece watched him clench his fists. *He's getting wound up. Time to defuse.*

He picked up his recorder and switched it on. "Why don't you tell me about her, Mr. Waskowski? I'll record our conversation so I have a record, if that's okay with you."

Waskowski shrugged and then nodded. "Sure. That's fine."

"So tell me all about your little sister. The more information I have, the better.

Kyle Waskowski took a deep breath and began talking.

# 23

## SUNDAY, JANUARY 12, 10:08 AM

I PUSHED OPEN the door to the bookshop. The bell tinkling overhead announced my entrance. Although to whom was a bit of a mystery, as the shop appeared to be empty.

Out of habit, I removed my hat and put my pipe in my coat pocket. Etiquette seems to be a thing of the past these days, and hats are routinely worn indoors. A definite no-no when it comes to hat etiquette, unless you happen to be a Muslim or Jewish man, or a woman.

My eyes took in the place. To the left was a desk, table, computer, a comfy-looking chair, and an iPad on a stand. On my right were several tables on which were stacked what at first glance appeared to be remaindered books. Straight ahead were the stacks. Rows of bookshelves. And beyond them was an open doorway.

The lighting was bright, and the shop looked clean. Not like most of the used bookstores I'd visited over the years.

I took a stroll among the stacks. The books were a mix of contemporary mainstream and romance. Lots of romance.

My stroll took me to a locked glass case along the wall not far from the desk.

The rare books. That is if the cousins followed the practice of the other used bookstores I'd visited over the years. Always the locked glass case containing the rare books with the even more rarefied prices.

I was perusing the titles when I became aware of the tap-tap of a woman's high-heeled shoes on the wood floor behind me. I turned, and there was Hester Galt.

"Good morning, Mr. Thurgood." She extended her hand, which I took in mine, and bowed over it.

She giggled. "Oh, my. A Victorian gentleman."

"I'm not sure about Victorian, but I strive to be a gentleman. And I thought you would appreciate the greeting.

"Oh, I did. My wife and I are passionate about Victoriana. Thank you for noticing and not thinking we're a couple of nuts."

"Aren't we all nuts, to some degree?"

"Goodness. A philosopher as well."

"Just an observer of the human condition."

"Well, Mr, Thurgood, there's a lot to observe, isn't there?"

"There is. And do call me Harry."

"Very well, Harry. I'm Hester."

"Charmed to make your acquaintance, my lady." And I bowed again.

She giggled and clapped her hands. "You are a delight. Augie will be sad to have missed meeting you like this."

"Another time."

"Yes, another time."

"I like your shop. A good arrangement. The books that will appeal to most people are here in front and the others, I assume, are through the doorway in the room beyond."

"Thank you. Yes, more books through the doorway. Science fiction, fantasy, non-fiction, and much more. But of lesser interest to the casual walk-in customer. We thought it made sense. I have the inventory list ready for you. Do you want a hard copy or is a digital one okay?"

"Digital is fine." I gave her my email, which she jotted down using what looked like a vintage Victorian era mechanical pencil.

"Is that a pencil an antique?"

"Yes, it is."

"So what spurred your interest in the Victorian era?"

"Literature. Augie and I both love Victorian era literature. Especially ghosts and vampires."

"Really? Why those two?"

"We think that the Victorians, because of the Industrial Revolution and scientific advancement, were both drawn to and repelled by the machine. The repulsion manifested itself in their fascination with ghosts and vampires and the afterlife. After all, ghosts and vampires conquer death, as it were, by supernatural means. Something science pooh-poohs. In *Dracula,* it isn't science that destroys the vampire, it's faith. And faith isn't scientific."

"Interesting. Very interesting."

"Victorian literature is fascinating."

"I'll have to put some books on my reading list."

"Augie and I are here if you need suggestions."

"Thank you."

"And speaking of books, if we default, what are you going to do with the inventory?"

"Good question. I have no desire to run a bookstore."

"And without most of our stock we couldn't keep the shop open."

"Then perhaps you sell the inventory for me and you get a cut of the profit for doing the selling."

"That could work."

"This is, of course, all hypothetical. You'll pay back the loan. Business is good, isn't it?"

"We've had a slow start, but traffic is growing, as are sales. Come tourist season, I think we'll see a big upturn in both traffic and purchases."

"Good to hear."

"You mentioned a reading list, so you are a reader?"

"Very much so. Always have at least one book in progress."

"What do you like?"

"Most genres. No romance and I'm not much into mainstream. I'm currently reading The Boom Town Saga."

"I've not heard of that. Who's the author?"

"Caleb Pirtle the third. He passed away, so the three books are all there is. Which is too bad. I love the main characters."

"The name sounds familiar. I think we have some coffee table books by him."

"He wrote several. He was a Texas native, so I thought reading the saga would help me to get a feel for my new home."

"Good idea."

Hester walked over to the desk, sat, tapped some keys on the computer, and when she stopped, said, "The inventory list is on its way to you."

"Thanks."

"And thank you for the loan."

"Can't ever have too much inventory."

"No, you can't."

I continued perusing the books in the case and was vaguely aware of the bell over the door ringing. A moment later, I felt arms encircle my chest from behind and a hot, slightly minty breath whispered in my ear, "Harry Thurgood. I love you."

On hearing the words, I knew who the person was. I turned around and was nose to nose with Scarlett Hayden. Her perfume was subtle and smelled a bit like cinnamon.

"Hello, Scarlett."

She said nothing. Merely kissed me. And the kiss wasn't particularly chaste.

When she pulled away, I said, "And good morning to you."

"It's been too long, Harry."

Hester said, "I take it you two know each other."

"Yes, we do," Scarlett confirmed.

I added, "But not in the biblical way."

Hester smiled. "I'm glad you clarified that."

I couldn't help but notice her eyes were devouring Scarlett, who slipped an arm around my waist.

Oblivious to the hunger in the bookshop owner's eyes, Scarlett said, "I was doing my darndest to get this man in my bed, and what's he do? Goes off and marries the Methodist minister. She must be okay, because now they have twins."

"Ember's more than okay."

"I should hope so. She had plenty of practice."

There was a puzzled look forming on Hester's face. But before I could say anything, Scarlett added, "Our little Ember used to be a porn star."

Hester's eyebrows shot up, and I could feel the heat rising on my face.

Scarlett laughed. "Stick around, Hester. Magnolia Bluff is a wild place. Don't let the placid surface fool you."

She gave me a squeeze and withdrew her arm from around my waist.

I cleared my throat. "Well, ladies, I'm going to say goodbye. Good to see you, Scarlett. And good to see you again, Hester. I'm off to see if I can catch the Queen's grand entrance."

Scarlett let loose a deep and throaty laugh.

Puzzlement settled in on Hester's face.

"I'll fill you in," Scarlett said to her. To me, she said goodbye and blew me a kiss.

Once on the sidewalk, I checked my watch. *If I hurry, I should just make it.*

# 24

## SUNDAY, JANUARY 12, 1:04 PM

At the head of the table sat Gunter Fight. To his right sat his wife, Mary Lou. To his left was his adopted daughter, Oralene, and to her left was the Reverend Adelbert Humphrey the fourth.

Also at the table were several members of Saint Luke's church council and trustee board.

Mary Lou asked the Reverend Humphrey to say grace, which he did with great unction.

Oralene gave him an unobtrusive nudge when he'd gone past the two-minute mark. She was, after all, hungry and didn't much care at the moment if God preserved the Congo rainforests from destruction or not.

The Reverend got the hint, brought his globetrotting back to Texas, and most importantly, implored the blessing of the good God on the food of which they were about to partake.

The amens said in response to Reverend Humphrey's prayer carried overtones of relief and gratefulness.

Oralene waited until Eliška and the extra hired help had finished serving the first course, corn bisque, to ask Humphrey if only gay people were our neighbors.

"Oh, no. Everyone is our neighbor. I focused on gay people this morning because there are those who were not in favor of lifting the ban. And now that it's been lifted, we want to make sure love rules the day."

"I doubt that will be a problem here at Saint Luke's," Mary Lou said.

"Mostly because there are no homosexuals in Magnolia Bluff," Maness Sebren, chairman of the trustee board, said.

"I hear they're at the college," Waymon Riggins, the chair of the finance committee, countered.

Sebren sniffed his disgust. "The college isn't Magnolia Bluff."

"Reverend Cole is trying to get them to come to church," church treasurer Euel Pinckney reminded everyone.

Reverend Humphrey, his voice very pious sounding, said, "Those who are without the light need the light."

Oralene thought about what her father would've said on all of this: *Sinners burn in hell. Homosexuals pervert God's natural order and will burn in the deepest pits of hell.* He always got a lot of amens.

She put a spoonful of soup in her mouth. *I was brought up in religion. It's nothing but a cesspool of sin and hypocrisy. And now Mother wants me to marry Reverend Humphrey and commit more sin and hypocrisy.*

Tipper Duvall's voice broke into Oralene's thoughts. "It was so good to see you at church today, Mrs. Fight."

There was a murmur of agreement around the table.

"It was good to be back," Mary Lou said. "Now, if everyone is finished with the soup, I'll have Eliška serve the salmon salad."

Oralene's eyes slid left and gazed at the simpering cleric by her side. *There must be a way to get what I want and not be tied to him.*

---

Reece Sovern sat at his desk comparing the statement of Kyle Waskowski with the six file folders of evidence from the Sheriff's department and the evidence the MBPD had so far compiled on the death of Kari Waskowski.

The statement Mr. Waskowski provided contained a lot of information, but Reece was uncertain as to what was useful and what wasn't.

But that was normal for an investigation. Most of the information police gathered ended up being of little to no use. Like putting together a five hundred piece puzzle with a hundred extra pieces that don't fit.

The brother had given them all manner of data regarding his sister, but virtually nothing on the cult group itself.

"So we know that Kari Lynn stopped going to church her senior year in high school, showed no interest in spiritual matters until she found the New Order of the Crimson Dawn, and had trouble finding a path in life," Reece recapitulated to himself.

He shook his head. "I guess she found a path in the end. Like we all do. The path that leads to death."

There was a knock on the door.

"Come in."

The door opened and one of the clerical staff poked her head in. "Captain wants you in his office, Reece."

"Thanks, EllieSue."

The door closed, and Reece looked at the ceiling. *What does he want now?*

He got up and walked down the hall to his boss's office.

"Hi, Cap. You wanted to see me?"

"Grab a seat."

Reece sat.

"Where are you at on our full moon killer case?"

Reece told him.

"We need to wrap this up quick. The DA is chewing the Sheriff's butt and I don't want him to start chewing the chief's. Because if he does, the chief will chew mine. And you know what that means?"

"Yes, sir, I do."

"I want this case solved pronto. Because if you solve it, then the others get solved too. A big win for the DA and for us. And the DA needs a big win. Election, you know. He needs a big win for *law enforcement*. Not civilians. Capiche?"

"Yeah, I capiche."

"Good. Now get out there and get us a win, Sergeant. Don't want to be directing traffic, do you?"

"No, sir."

Reece left and headed back to his office. Once there, he shook his head. Grabbed his hat and coat, muttered, "Politics. Goddamn politics," and headed for his car.

# 25

## SUNDAY, JANUARY 12, 1:31 PM

Ember was ecstatic, and I was happy for her. Three students, a young man and two young women, professed their faith in Christ at her open air meeting on the Burnet College campus.

"There were fifteen waiting for me when I got there," she said. "Jim Conroy set up the speaker's platform and made sure there were batteries in the megaphone, although I didn't need to use it."

"Wonderful, honey. So now what?"

"Two haven't ever been baptized. So I'll baptize them at church. The other student was baptized as a Catholic."

"Catholic? Why did he or she—"

"She."

"Why did she decide to become a Methodist?"

"She's not sure she wants to become a Methodist, but she realized she needed something in her life other than sex, drugs, and booze. She said my story inspired her."

"That is fantastic. I'm glad for you."

"I am so very glad that my life of sin can bring people to Christ. They just need to see how empty they are."

We were in the family room. A fire was burning in the fireplace, and I was holding Max, who'd finished nursing. Monette was hanging on. She's a little milk hound.

Both Princess and Wilbur were curled up by the fire, but each was occupying his and her own corner of the hearthrug.

A beautiful picture of the happy little modestly wealthy family's domestic life. A communist or socialist I am not. I like money. Lots of it. I like what it gives to me and mine in the way of not only the necessities of life but also the comforts and even some of the luxuries of life.

Money is my servant, not my master. There were times before Em where I purposefully lived as a poor person. Just to prove to myself that my money didn't control me.

Em talks a lot about living simply and not needing a lot of money. But I'm happy to report that I'm slowly corrupting my ascetic little wife.

Ember continued. "Maybe I should let Adelbert take the Sunday pulpit at Saint Luke's and I'll preach at the college."

"Not a good plan, my little chickadee."

"Why not?"

"The pulpit is what you are getting paid to occupy. So occupy it. The pulpit is where your strength lies. Use it to advocate your vision. Barnstorming for Jesus is a side activity. Best keep it there."

"But it was so exhilarating to hear those students—"

"Nope. They aren't paying you. Your parishioners are, and so they get you first."

"You're right. They do and they should. But I will make time for the college. They are hungering for meaning, for purpose. They want a cause to believe in."

"Maybe Friday afternoon or Saturday morning."

"Good idea, Harry."

"Thank you. Now is little Miss Piggy done? I'm hungry."

---

By the time we got to Olivia's, the after church crowd was pretty much gone. As usual, she had our steaming hot pies on our table not more than five minutes after our sitters had begun warming the booth seats. A vegetarian special for Em and a double pepperoni for me. There was a bottle of chianti to help wash the food down.

How she knows what we want is a mystery. There's some psychic connection there, but what it is exactly beats me.

"So, were you able to watch the Queen's grand entrance?"

I drank wine, nodded, and took a bite of pizza. After that bite was on its way to my stomach, I said, "I was wondering if they were going to play 'The Arrival of the Queen of Sheba' or 'Zadok the Priest'."

"I don't know either of those songs."

"The first is an orchestral piece from Handel's oratorio *Solomon*. The second is one of the coronation anthems for the British monarch, also written by Handel."

I played a few bars of "The Arrival of the Queen of Sheba" on my phone, then sang the lines from the anthem: "God save the Queen! Long live the Queen! God save the Queen!/May the Queen live for ever."

"Oh my God, Harry. I hope she doesn't live forever."

"All I can say is that your God is doing a fine job of keeping her breathing."

"Now wait one minute, Mister."

I cut her off. "Isn't he omnipotent?"

"Oh, no. You aren't getting me entangled in that predestination stuff. Uh-uh."

"Okay. Boy, this pizza sure is good."

Em laughed. "Yes, it is. So music and theology aside, was she there?"

"Yes, she was. In all of her regal splendor. She entered the building on Gunter's arm and slowly paraded down the central aisle, bestowing smiles on the peons and shaking hands with a few of the more important peons. Following in her wake were four of the Hats. Not sure why they were there. Perhaps they were her ladies-in-waiting."

"Good grief."

"It was almost farcical. And Humpty Dumpty went on for seven minutes, I timed him, extolling the virtues of the Fights, and Mary Lou in particular."

"Seriously?"

"Yep. That woman has a problem. A big problem."

"At least with her back at the church, it will be easier to keep an eye on her."

"True that."

"And Adelbert's message?"

"Some snoozer about… Gee, I'm not sure. He did say 'love' ninety-six times. I counted them."

I watched Em roll her eyes and laughed at her antics.

"So, when are you returning to the pulpit?"

"This coming Sunday."

"And you'll be back at work starting Tuesday?"

"Tomorrow."

"I thought Monday was your day off."

"I've had five weeks of days off, Mister."

"Okay. Enjoy."

I ate pizza for a minute before asking, "Since you're still off work, when we're done here, do you want to go home and get in some practice for number three?"

"Maybe we should get a doggie bag."

"Good idea."

# 26

## SUNDAY, JANUARY 12, 3:08 PM

Reece Sovern put the last bite of his chicken slider in his mouth, and when it was gone sucked down the last of his Dr. Pepper.

He looked at the time on his phone. *GJ should have something by now.* He tapped out a text asking how things were going.

In a moment, one came back with the word *calling*.

His phone rang and he answered, "How's my best investigator doing?"

"I'm your only investigator."

"So. You're still the best."

"Aw, man. Thanks, Sarge. You're the best, too."

"Found anything useful?"

"Sure have. Was going to call when I got your text."

"Okay. Spill it. Don't keep me in suspense. Briggs is chewing my butt."

"Oh, man. Okay. Here goes. She was employed as a stocker in a grocery story. Tischler's."

"Full time?"

"Yes. Her social life was not very active. Spent time with friends perhaps once a month. I found her laptop in her room and we lucked out: she didn't password protect it. So I took a good look at what her online life was like. Pretty boring, for the most part. About as interesting as her social life.

"However, there's one site she visited repeatedly. It's called New Order of the Crimson Dawn and it's run by a Countess Anastasija and a Countess Izolda."

Reece asked her to spell the names for him. After she did, he said, "Go on. Anything else?"

"There was an email exchange. The last email was an invitation to partake in a Crimson Dawn festival in Magnolia Bluff."

"Did the email say where in Magnolia Bluff the festival was to be held?"

"No."

"So how did our victim know where to go?"

"Perhaps one of those countesses called her. Phone number is required on the application form."

"I don't recall seeing any of this material in what we got from Buck's people. I wonder why?"

"Good question, Sarge."

"Anything else?"

"That's the most important. So far anyway. I'm going to talk to a few more people. Should be home tonight or tomorrow."

"Keep me posted."

"Will do."

Reece ended the call and leaned back in the car seat. This was an important break, and he knew it. The important question, though, was it enough to get them to first base.

## 27

### SUNDAY, JANUARY 12, 4:37 PM

REECE SAT at his desk and picked up the folder that contained the information on Tessa Wang, the Full Moon Killer's first victim.

Her naked body had been found in Rockvale Cemetery, which was quite remarkable given the two sets of fences the killer had to go through to get into the cemetery, the last vestige of the once thriving community of Rockvale, Texas.

Deputy Investigator Phil West had interviewed Ms. Wang's parents in Los Angeles, but found them completely puzzled why she would be in Texas. She'd always talked about going to Hawaii, her mother had told the DI.

The twenty-eight-year-old woman, according to her boss at the art store where she worked, had simply asked him not to schedule her from the second through the fifth of July. She hadn't told family or friends that she'd be gone.

A sticky note on the case file had the words:

Full Moon July 3rd

written on it.

The woman's body was badly decomposed. It had been lying

in the cemetery for six weeks. The Rangers, combing through missing person reports, had finally made the identification for the Burnet County Sheriff Department's Criminal Investigations unit.

Reece pulled up a website listing the full moon dates for the county.

*Two in August. The first and the thirtieth. Sturgeon Moon and Blue Moon. But there was only one victim in August.*

He looked through the folders. Victim number two. Twenty-year-old Peter Gargano from Cleveland, Ohio. Body found on the second of August in the cemetery of Naruna Baptist Church. ME gave time of death between nine and ten on the night of the first.

Another sticky note had the full moon date on it.

Reece set the folder aside and picked up the next one.

*The third victim was killed on the night of September's full moon. Is there another body out there somewhere for August's Blue Moon? God, I hope not.*

He repositioned his glasses on the top of his nose, took out an emerald green corona from the desk drawer, removed the cellophane, and sank his teeth into it.

The next victim was from Norman, Oklahoma. Tippah Colbert. A twenty-three-year-old Chickasaw woman. She worked as a clerk in the Chickasaw Nation Legislative Department.

*Victims all naked. No personal effects found. No cell phone. No laptop, iPad, or desktop PC (not that anyone has one anymore). And no mention of this New Order of the Crimson Dawn. Pretty efficient scrubbing of evidence. That's enough to get the imagination going. What killer is that damn efficient?*

*If it wasn't for Kari Waskowski leaving her laptop in her room instead of taking it with her, we still wouldn't know about this online cult group they were all involved in.*

Reece looked at his watch and decided a drive out to the Thurgood-Cole residence might yield some insight.

## 28

### SUNDAY, JANUARY 12, 5:47 PM

After our practice run for Cole-Thurgood number three, Em and I were dressing into something much more presentable than our birthday suits in order to go out and get something to eat when I heard the doorbell.

"You expecting anyone?"

Em shook her head.

"Me neither." I picked up my phone and looked at the security app. The camera showed me that our favorite police investigator was at the door.

"It's Reece. Wonder what he wants? I'll be back."

I took the stairs and reached the door as the bell sounded a second time. I looked through the one-way glass panel to make sure it was Reece and it was.

*If he's here to talk about the case, he better hope Briggs doesn't have someone watching the house.*

I opened the door. "Good afternoon, Sarge. Come in."

"Hi, Harry. I'd like to chat. Do you have a few minutes? You and the Reverend?"

"We were just going out to eat. Join us?"

"Oh, uh, no. I couldn't. I'll come back another time. Tomorrow okay?"

"No. Seriously. Join us. Bring Hetta, too."

"It's about the case."

"Of course it is." I had a grin on my face. "Text Hetta and tell her we'll be there in fifteen minutes to pick her up."

"I feel like I'm crashing a party."

"Nonsense. Wait here."

I turned to go up the stairs, and there was Princess. Guarding the gate, so to speak. I told her Reece was a friend and asked him to call her. When he did, I told her to go. Which she did, albeit cautiously.

Up the stairs I went. In the bedroom, I told Em we had a slight change in plans.

"Sure. Hetta's nice," Em said.

I made certain everything was set, so I looked my best (yes, I know, I'm a bit vain), and headed back downstairs with Em in tow.

Reece and Princess appeared to be old friends.

After a brief discussion, we agreed to meet at O'Gara's. Reece felt that if he drove separately, should word get back to Briggs, our meeting would appear to be accidental.

The whole thing made me think of high school. For Reece's sake, I agreed to the subterfuge.

---

We arrived at O'Gara's a good ten minutes ahead of our guests. I greeted Gill Simmons, the owner, and made a quip on the lack of patrons.

Gill, completely deadpan, said, "The Baptists have Sunday evening services."

I chuckled while directing Em to a booth in a back corner. We settled in and Fleur Beauchamp, Gill's twenty-something girlfriend, arrived to take our orders. A French 75 mocktail for Em and a Martinez for me.

Reece and Hetta joined us, and when Fleur delivered our

drinks, took their order. Iced sweet tea for Hetta and a Shiner Bock for Reece. And we all put in orders for burgers and fries.

I took a sip of my drink, savored it for a moment, and then said, "Okay, Reece, what's up?"

He pushed his glasses back up to the top of his nose. "We got a break in the case. Our victim left her laptop in the room she was renting, and GJ was able to go through it because it wasn't locked or password protected."

Fleur dropped off the drinks for the Soverns.

When she was gone, I said, "That is a lucky break for you."

Reece drank beer, nodded, and said, "Tell me about it. So we find out our victim was involved in some kind of cult group that appears to be based right here in Magnolia Bluff. At least that's where the victim was told the festival and special ritual would be conducted."

"And you're assuming the others were told to come here as well."

Reece nodded. "She didn't stay at the B and B, or Cozy Corners. I have a list of hotels, motels, bed and breakfasts, internet rental places, and private rooms or homes available for short-term stay within a twenty-five mile radius to call and hopefully find out where she stayed. And now that we have a name, I can check rental car companies."

I nodded my head in agreement. "Probably flew into Dallas or Austin."

"Right."

"So why do you want to talk to us?" Ember asked. "It looks like you have everything under control."

Fleur arrived with our food, asked if we needed anything, and with four negatives, she said, "Enjoy," and left.

In between French fries, Reece answered Ember's question, which was my question too.

"I would like you, Reverend, to take a look at this website." Reece tapped on his phone and handed it to Em. I looked over her shoulder.

She read, scrolled, read some more, tapped to a new page, read some more, and after looking at several pages and reading the About Us, she handed the phone back to Reece.

"What can you tell me?" he asked. "Based on your experience."

Ember thought a moment, before saying, "It's all in circles and riddles. They obviously think they've found the fountain of youth. Or at least want the visitor to think so. At the same time, it's all wrapped up in a lot of death language and that disturbs me. The last thing we need is for another kook to encourage people to commit suicide."

"Our victims didn't commit suicide," Reece said. "They were murdered."

Ember popped a fry into her mouth and nodded in agreement. "True. Are you sure the recent victim was lured here by this website?"

"Not the website so much as whoever is behind the website."

"A spider and fly approach to serial killing," I said.

A grim smile appeared on Reece's face. "Yeah. Something like that."

"Can you track down who's hosting the website? Who owns the domain name? Stuff like that?"

"Yes. Briggs and the chief have asked the Rangers for help on the cyber end."

"Good," I said. "Unless this person is very smart, that should get you your perp."

"Should," Reece agreed.

His phone dinged. He looked at it, and after a moment, smiled.

"Good news?" I asked.

He smiled. "A will just surfaced for one of the victims. The sole beneficiary is the New Order of the Crimson Dawn."

# 29

## SUNDAY, JANUARY 12, 7:02 PM

"WELL, Sarge, I think you may have found your motive," I said, before taking a bite of my burger.

"I think you're right," he said. "Con the suckers, get them to name this nut group in the will, then kill 'em off and cash in."

"That's brutal," Em said.

"We live in a brutal world, Reverend," Reece explained.

"When I was a kid, it wasn't like that," Hetta said. "At least here in the Bluff. But things slowly started to change. First with those murders every May, and now pretty much somebody local or visiting dying every month. It's become a very brutal world."

"In one sense, yes," I said, "but in another, no."

"What do you mean?" Reece asked.

"What we are seeing here in Magnolia Bluff is simply the playing out of what has probably been simmering beneath the surface for generations. Our present society has thrown restraint to the wind. Once that happened, it opened the gate for violence to be exercised without regard for the consequences."

"That's pretty philosophical," Reece said.

Ember disagreed. "For the longest time, Christian values governed society. There was etiquette, based on those Christian values, to tell us how to behave with one another, how to be respectful and polite towards each other. The nasty parts of life, while they existed, were very much kept in the closet. People 'destroyed' each other socially. With words. Although even that was frowned upon.

"Today, however, if we don't like something, we riot, destroy property, and kill others. There is no respect for others. It is all about me.

"We are inundated with violence. Video games. Comic books. TV. Movies. BDSM is now quite accepted, when not that long ago it wasn't even talked about. Violence is everywhere. So I'm not surprised that we are seeing these murders. People now feel they can act on what in the past they could only imagine."

Reece's face was thoughtful as he chewed his bite of burger.

Hetta said, "I agree, Ember. It's all messed up. There are no inhibitions anymore. Nothing practical is taught in school. It's nothing but sex. And violence isn't tolerated, but, as you point out, our society has become very violent because violence is everywhere. It's a mess. No order. No stability."

"What I can't figure out is what does this cult group offer to the suckers to pull them in?" Reece said. "I don't see it."

"I don't disagree with you, Reece," Ember said. "The website is pretty nebulous. Eternal life from eternal death. What does that mean?"

"Sounds kind of goth to me," I said. "The goth movement is all into death."

Ember's face was thoughtful. Finally she said, "True. But this group is offering life out of or through death. It's almost Christian. In Christ, I'm dead to the world and alive to Him. To die is gain. But this group is saying you can actually live by dying. An oxymoron to be certain. But then, so is a lot of Christian thought."

Reece stroked his chin for a moment, then said, "Kind of sounds like some of the vampire crap the boys were into for a while."

"And Annie Kate, too," Hetta said. "Those *Twilight* books she was reading."

"Also of interest," I began, "there are vampire lifestylers. People who think they're vampires. And some even drink blood."

"Oh, that's gross," Hetta said.

"Where the hell do you come up with this stuff?" Reece asked.

I shrugged. "I read. There was quite a big case up in Minneapolis some years ago. A group of these vampire wannabes went off the rails and were killing people. That private detective who came here for the fundraising concert? Justinia Wright? She apparently had a hand in solving that one."

Reece looked skeptical. "Are you saying we have those nut jobs down here? In Magnolia Bluff?"

"Don't know. Just mentioned it. Fits, though. Eternal life though eternal death."

Hetta smiled. "Reece is very down to earth. Practical. He's not given to flights of fancy."

Reece glanced at his wife. "I'm a practical man because this is a practical world. Vampires. Sheesh."

I smiled to myself. Reece is a bulldog. All he lacks is imagination.

# 30

## SUNDAY, JANUARY 12, 9:02 PM

Reece dropped his wife off at home and then drove on to the station. He wanted to jot down notes from his conversation with Harry and Ember.

He found it difficult to believe that anything so wacky as vampire lifestylers could be in Magnolia Bluff. Sure, there were a lot of kooks in the world, but people who thought they were vampires?

That's the nutty stuff you'd find in New York City, or Seattle, or even Houston. But not in Magnolia Bluff.

He took the cellophane off of an emerald green corona and got his teeth into it.

*Then again, there is the college,* he mused. *Lots of whack jobs out there.*

Nevertheless, he wrote down everything the minister and the coffee shop owner had said, and when finished read through the notes.

"The cult group somehow cons the suckers into joining," he muttered. "Then they get the suckers to name them as sole beneficiary in their wills. And finally, the cult people kill off the suckers and cask in on their wills."

Reece thought that over for a bit. Suddenly he asked himself, "But did any of our victims have money?"

He began paging through the file folders to see if the Sheriff's CI unit had gotten bank information. After fifteen minutes, he tossed the last folder onto the pile.

"Of course they didn't. But they will now. Nothing like a will to focus attention on money. Speaking of which…"

He fired off a text to GJ.

Within three minutes, he had her answer:

Bank website was bookmarked on her laptop. Couldn't get in because of the password. There was no autofill. Will stop at the bank tomorrow, but will probably need a warrant.

What bank?

Wells Fargo

He texted back a thanks and that he'd start the ball rolling on a warrant.

Lucky break. A national bank like that, they'd be able to get the information locally.

Reece felt confident the will angle was the reason for the killings. *Regardless of the folderol used to get the suckers in. After all, most murders occur because of money. And these killings were shaping up to be no different.*

---

Em and I were sitting by the fire. She was drinking tea and I coffee. I filled my pipe and lit it. Nothing like a bowl of the sacred leaf. Wilbur and Princess were on the hearthrug. The twins were sleeping upstairs in their room.

"Seems like a very complex ruse to get people to name the Crimson Dawn in their wills," Em said.

"Maybe. Maybe not. All depends if it works."

"Did any of the victims possess significant wealth?"

I puffed on my pipe and said, "Don't know."

"If they didn't, then it sure seems like a lot of bother over nothing."

"I suppose. Then again, it could be they are purposely targeting people with little money so that the wills don't get challenged."

"Still. They are going to have to con and kill an awful lot of people to make any serious money."

"And maybe they don't mind. Maybe they're actually into the killing and the money is just secondary."

"That's sick."

"Didn't say it wasn't."

"And the risk of getting caught. That must be pretty high."

"I'm guessing they don't stay in any one place for too long. Moving around is the best way to not get caught."

"Seven victims at one a month means they've been here at least seven months."

"True. And at this point, the perp is possibly looking at winding up shop here and moving on. He has to know he now has the MBPD after him, as well as the sheriff's department. With the possibility that the Rangers might get actively involved or the FBI, if it's shown that kidnapping is involved."

"If he does move on, then these murders might go unsolved."

"Might."

Em was quiet. I had nothing to say, so I puffed on my pipe, drank coffee, and stared at the fire.

"Harry, I wonder if Reece should check out all the people who've lived in town less than a year."

"Launching a witch hunt on newcomers?"

"No. But if the murders started seven months ago, it's likely that's when the killer moved to town."

"Makes sense. Have to check the county, too, because the killer might not live in Magnolia Bluff."

"I'll suggest it to Reece tomorrow."

"I hope it doesn't turn into a witch hunt."

"He's just checking. Routine work."

"I suppose."

Em drank tea and I gazed at the fire.

After some time, I said, "Do you know what bothers me the most about these killings?"

"No. Tell me."

"The missing livers."

## 31

SUNDAY, JANUARY 12, 10:42 PM

THE DOOR next to the loading dock wasn't locked. Oralene Fight knew it wouldn't be. They were expecting her. The knob turned in her hand, the door opened, and she stepped in out of the heavy mist.

Meeting her at the door was her brother, Lofton.

"Where's John-John?" Oralene demanded. "And why don't you get some lights in this place?"

"He's praying with one of the church members."

"Is he doing a Pa?"

"I don't know, O."

"How long have they been praying?"

"Half an hour."

Oralene shook her head. "He's going to get himself in trouble, he is."

"He's getting forty to fifty people to show up every Sunday."

"I guess that's good. Mama still singing?"

"Everyone but you."

"Well, I have to be with Mother Fight. She's rich. And right now that's the side my bread's buttered on."

Oralene heard a door open and saw a bright shaft of light. In a moment, a young woman, with long blonde hair and a chest that fought the confines of her jacket, walked briskly past them and out the back door. In a minute, her oldest brother, John-John, joined them.

"Hello, O. Haven't seen you in a while. Sure miss your voice Sunday mornings."

"I have to be with Mother Fight."

"There is much wickedness in that one."

"There's also a lot of money with her."

"The love of money—"

"Can it, John-John. Don't be talking to me about sin. How many special prayer meetings do you hold each week? You're going down the road Pa went down."

"I am not."

"Don't lie to me. I'm your sister. I know man sin when I see it *and* smell it. Now I need to talk business."

Lofton said, "We built a kind of cabin over here, O. Come on, let me show you."

Oralene and John-John followed their younger brother to the boxy structure that was some fifteen to twenty feet away from the office and the old employee's lavatory.

Lofton opened the door. "This is the living room. Straight ahead is the dining room and kitchen. There, just before the hall, is the coat closet. Then down the hall are two bedrooms. When we get more money, we'll hire a plumber to get us running water in the kitchen."

"Kind of cozy," Oralene said.

"It works," John-John said. "Saves on rent."

"And that's good," Oralene added.

"So why are you here, O?" John-John asked.

"Have a seat, O," Lofton said.

Oralene sat in a very used overstuffed chair. Her brothers pulled up chairs facing her to form a triangle.

"There is sin again," Oralene said, "and it needs to be purged."

"In our family?" John-John asked.

"Indirectly. Mother Fight wants me to marry the Reverend Adelbert Humphrey."

"Marry a minister?" Lofton said. "That's wonderful, O."

"He's a Sodomite. His family has position, money, and power. And so Mother Fight doesn't care if he's a Sodomite or not. All she cares about is what he can provide me and, by extension, her. But we care that he's an enemy of God, don't we? Remember what Pa said?"

Her brothers nodded their heads.

"We know Sodomites are hated by God. Sinful perversions of His righteous image. Do we not?"

Again, the brothers nodded their agreement.

But after a moment, John-John said, "I don't know, O. The last time didn't go so well."

"What do you mean?"

"You know. Lofton was arrested and almost convicted—"

"But I wasn't. That lawyer Mr. Thurgood paid for did real good getting me off."

Oralene tapped her right foot. *He is going soft for sure. Happens when a righteous man starts poking around in the serpent's den.*

She stood, hands on hips. "Very true, Lofton. So I want to know, John Reston, what do you mean it didn't go well? God spared us one and all. He has blessed us. We excised the sin. Cut it out of the Body of Christ, and He has blessed us. You and this church and me with Mother Fight. Mama has a good job and can provide for the little ones. Lofton's not in prison. What do you mean 'last time didn't go so well'?"

John-John started to speak, but Oralene cut him off. "We are again faced with sin. *I* am faced with sin. And you...," she thrust her finger in his face, "God's anointed prophet, His righteous servant, must deliver me from the hands of the Evil One."

She sat down and glared at her brother.

"I'm not sure, O. Can't you tell Mrs. Fight no?"

"No one tells Mrs. Fight anything. No, I can't tell her *no*. Are you refusing to help your sister in need, John-John?"

"Well, uh—"

"You realize, Jael, who did the work of the Lord, was God's second choice. He chose her only because there were no righteous men. Men who would bravely stand in the strength of the Lord. Are you, the Lord's servant, a coward?"

"I'm not, O!" Lofton cried out.

"I know you aren't, my faithful and loyal brother. Are you, John-John, taking the path Pa took? Are you going to shirk your duty for the pleasures of the flesh?"

Oralene watched the pain on her brother's face. She feared the day would soon come when she wouldn't be able to manipulate him to do her bidding. And perhaps the day was already here.

"Let me think about it, O. This one's different. I need to think about it."

Oralene stood. "Very well, John-John. But I need your answer soon. Very soon. Once Mother Fight decides something, she won't wait. And I am not going to be tied to a Sodomite. That is sin even God won't forgive."

Lofton stood. "I'll walk with you to the door, O."

Oralene left the little cabin with her brother, crossed the floor, and stepped out of the back door into the misty night air.

"Don't worry, O. I'm here for you."

"Thank you, Lofton. I fear your brother is getting soft. Sin does that. It did it to Pa."

"I know. I tell him, but he won't listen."

"Goodnight, Lofton." She kissed her brother on the cheek.

"Goodnight, O."

Oralene walked to her car and got in. *The day has come. There are no righteous men in the land.*

She started the big Cadillac. *Jael must rise up. Hammer and tent peg in her hand.*

# 32

## MONDAY, JANUARY 13, 7:11 AM

Reece Sovern was sitting at a table in the Sheriff's wing of the courthouse with Deputy Detective Phil West, who was in charge of the investigation on the Sheriff's side of the joint investigation. Also present were Captain Davis Briggs and Captain Arthur Helier of the Sheriff's CI unit.

Deputy Detective West began the meeting. "Today is the first full moon of the year. This killer has completely eluded us and left us wondering why he's killing these people. Now, thanks to the surfacing of the will of Alyssa Marsh, who was victim number six, we at least feel confident we have a motive. In addition, the recovery of Ms. Waskowski's laptop has given us a starting point to discover who our killer is."

Captain Briggs said, "We're getting a warrant to access Ms. Waskowski's bank accounts, and our officer in Chicago is checking to see if the victim had a will."

"The problem is who is this person who is killing these people?" Captain Helier said. "Until we determine who the perp is, get a profile on him, or her, none of this other stuff matters."

"Perhaps not," Briggs said, "but we don't know if the key clue isn't already lying somewhere in this other stuff unless we look for it."

Helier shrugged.

Deputy Detective West said, "I think if we divide up the tasks, we can cover more ground faster."

Reece nodded. "Good plan. We need to look into this cult and identify the actual people behind it. So we understand who we are dealing with. We also need to explore the money end to determine if that's the actual motive. We need to find out if any of the other victims had a will and gave these kooks money."

"I agree," West said. "Since the will came to us, I propose we explore the potential money motive. The Rangers are working on tracking down who is behind the website. I'll tell our contact person to pass the info they get onto you. Are you okay with that arrangement, Sergeant?"

Reece wasn't okay with it, but rather than create an inter-departmental brouhaha, he said, "Sure. Sounds good."

"And of course, we share all information with each other."

"Of course," Reece said.

---

On the walk back to the City Hall and the Police Station, Briggs said, "We got the crappy end of the stick. You realize that, don't you, Sergeant?"

Reece was perturbed. *Does this guy think I'm a moron? I may have been born at night, but it wasn't last night. Sheesh.*

To Briggs, he said, "I do. But I didn't think arguing with them would get us anywhere."

"Probably not. If I wasn't the new kid on the block, I would have pushed for us to take the money end. But this is what I want you to do, Sergeant. You have GJ track down the money end when she gets back. And while she's in Chicago, she might as well see what she can find. Got it?"

"Got it."

"Information sharing is fine. But I don't know these guys. How good they are. Blanton's a politico, and I don't trust politicians. How many of those deputies are political hirings? How many?"

Reece shrugged.

"Exactly. So you and GJ quietly explore the money end. We'll see if we can't bust this thing wide open before those county boys even reach first base. Capiche?"

"I capiche, Captain."

"Good. And keep those damn civilians out of it. You hear?"

"Loud and clear."

"Good. No nosy nob is taking away anything from us. We get the glory. Got it?"

Reece made a noise to indicate he heard his boss. To himself he said, *I'm willing to wager a bottle of Cowboy whiskey that it will be a nosy nob that gets the glory.*

# 33

## MONDAY, JANUARY 13, 7:57 AM

THE MOONLIGHT white metallic Mercedes-Maybach S680 pulled into the driveway of the dingy gray-white clapboard farmhouse.

The car took the once graveled drive at a very slow speed, the driver apparently wanting to minimize the amount of mud splatter on the quarter of a million dollar vehicle.

Finally, the sedan pulled to a stop before the porch steps of the house. After shutting off the engine, the woman opened the car door and stepped out. She wore an ankle-length, fitted waist, white coat with large black buttons running down the front. The wide brim white hat was pulled low to hide most of her face.

From the passenger side of the car, the woman retrieved two plastic bags and walked up to the front door, which she unlocked, and entered the house.

To the left was the living room. To the right, a door and, next to the door, a staircase. Straight ahead, down the short hall, and through another door, was the kitchen.

The woman walked to the kitchen and put the bags on the counter. Then turned around, retraced her steps, and ascended the stairs to the second floor. Upon reaching the landing, she turned left and entered a room.

In a thick accent, she said, "Are you hungry?"

The young woman, handcuffed to the bed frame and sitting on the floor, looked at her through half-closed eyes and nodded.

"Zoon, you vill leev forever ant ve vill leev tru you."

The woman returned to the kitchen, took the items out of the bags, and made a pot of oatmeal. She added nuts, raisins, marijuana, and a drug called Phrancinol. She gave it all a stir, dished some into a bowl, added a spoon, and took the bowl to the young woman.

After she was satisfied the young woman would eat the oatmeal, she went downstairs and sat in the living room. Twenty minutes later, she returned to the room. The young woman was lying on the bed. The bowl and spoon were on the floor.

The woman picked them up and took them down to the kitchen, where she washed and dried them.

Next, she filled a pitcher and glass with water and took them back upstairs to the prisoner.

She stood watching the figure in the bed. Then softly said, "Eternal life from eternal death."

There was no response from the captive, and the woman left.

She locked the front door to the old house, got into her car, drove slowly down the drive, and turned onto the paved road. Once on the road, the Mercedes-Maybach shot down the highway, leaving the old farmhouse quickly behind.

## 34

MONDAY, JANUARY 13, 8:04 AM

THE REVEREND EMBER Cole sat at her desk and looked around her spartan office and smiled. Her first day back on the job since she took her maternity leave. And it felt good.

She'd made a schedule so that Clara knew when to expect her home to nurse the twins. At first, Ember thought she'd pump milk and Clara could feed them. But she soon realized she'd miss her babies too much. So she arranged her schedule so she could be home at feeding time.

Today, she'd scheduled time to talk with members of the church council and with Reverend Humphrey. She hadn't been gone that long, but she wanted to touch base and make sure everything was okay. And perhaps surprise a few of them.

There was a knock on the door.

"Come in."

The Reverend Adelbert Humphrey the fourth, entered.

"Good morning, Reverend Cole. You wished to confer with me?"

Ember blinked at the sight of the dandified cleric.

In his hands was a short royal blue top hat of sorts with a brim that rolled up on the sides. The hat matched his coat, and he had buttoned the top button. Underneath the coat was a vest that was a riot of every hue of the rainbow. His shirt was white and the great knot of a tie at his throat was an electric pink. His slacks were a light gray with a dark gray stripe down the sides. On his feet were a pair of black Congress Gaiters. He wore grey gloves.

She recovered and hoped she hadn't stared too long at the sight of the cleric.

"Uh, yes. Have a seat."

Humphrey bowed to her and sat.

"I want to thank you for your service while I've been on maternity leave."

"You are very welcome. It is a joy to serve the Lord, is it not?"

"Yes, it very much is. I wanted to tell you first thing so you can make plans. I've asked the bishop to re-assign you."

"I'm sorry. You did what?"

"I've asked the bishop to reassign you."

"But what… I mean how…"

"It's nothing you've done. And I will give you a good review for your time here. But we both know you are a pawn in someone's chess game. Not one of my origin, to be sure. But unfortunately, it is one I'm forced to play."

"I don't understand."

"Oh, I'm sure you do."

Humphrey stared at Ember, and then he smiled. "You, Ms. Cole, are making a grave mistake. A very grave mistake."

"No, I don't think I am. Otherwise, I wouldn't have done what I did. There's a church in the district of thirty-five members that has an open pulpit. You will make them a fabulous interim pastor. And who knows, perhaps a permanent one. Possibly on a circuit with a larger church."

Humphrey stood. "Well! We shall see about this. I have connections, you do realize."

"So I've heard. The bishop is close to retirement. I doubt he cares a whole lot about connections."

"Well!"

And the Reverend Adelbert Humphrey the fourth, stormed out of Ember's office.

# 35

## MONDAY, JANUARY 13, 9:17 AM

THE WHITE MERCEDES-MAYBACH pulled into the parking lot of Saint Luke's United Methodist Church. A white-coated Tipper Duvall, Saint Luke's Lay Leader, exited the vehicle and walked briskly to the back door of the church, entered, and made her way to the church offices.

She asked Larrilyn Hammer, the receptionist and secretary, if Reverend Cole was in.

"Yes, she's expecting you," the secretary replied.

Tipper swept into the office without knocking.

"Good morning, Reverend."

"Good morning, Tipper. Have a seat."

Tipper removed her coat and laid it over the back of one of the chairs facing the minister's desk and sat in the other.

"Might get a sunny day today." To herself, she said, *She would do herself a favor by dressing in something other than black all the time.*

"That would be nice."

"How are the little ones?"

"Doing well, thank you."

"So, what is on the agenda this morning? I'm rather surprised to see you end your maternity leave so soon."

"I think you and I both know why I'm here."

"You're bored."

Tipper saw a smile appear on Ember's face.

"That's true in part. With Harry hiring a cook, housekeeper, and nanny, I have little to do. So I might as well come back to work. I'll go home when it's time to feed the twins. It's very nice to be able to set my own schedule."

"I'm sure it is. So what's the other part?"

"Mrs. Fight."

"Why would Mrs. Fight be a reason for you to end your maternity leave?"

"Tipper, you and I have been friendly. But you've made it clear we aren't friends. I'm still the outsider. A carpetbagger I believe you called me. I'm not one of you. I believe those were your words."

"I, uh, I—" Tipper stopped when Ember raised her hand.

"I'm not blind. Nor am I naïve. Nevertheless, regardless of how you feel towards me, you are my lay leader and we are going to work together for the good of this church in spite of Mrs. Fight's return."

"I don't understand what you mean. The Fights are loyal supporters of this church."

"They give money, yes. They control the governance for the most part. But they are supporters of their own interests. Not the interests of the church.

"Last year my husband gave more money than the Fights did in the previous five years. Because of him, we have more money than we've figured out how to spend. Yet there is still talk of removing me."

"Well, you see—"

"I do see, Tipper. And when the gossip starts getting around that the Fights no longer fill the coffers to overflowing, not that they ever did, I think Mary Lou and Gunter will be has beens."

Tipper closed her eyes. *I don't get what's happened to her, but*

*Mary Lou sure didn't anticipate this change in the strumpet. I need to tell her ASAP she is going to have a big fight on her hands.*

She opened her eyes. "Look, Reverend, Ember, I think perhaps you misunderstand—"

"No, I don't. I fully understand. And when you leave in a few minutes, you can tell Mrs. Fight that I've asked the bishop to reassign Reverend Humphrey."

"You what? You can't. That's a council decision."

"Even so, I did. And I do believe the bishop will honor my request and send us a replacement. This time, a replacement who will be more in line with the work and mission of this church instead of special interest groups."

"I see. You talk about the Fights and their money, but aren't you doing the same?"

"As the Good Book says, wise as a serpent and gentle as a dove."

Tipper watched Ember stand. She wasn't a tall woman, but she sure as heck was displaying plenty of presence. *What on earth has gotten into her?*

"Have a blessed day, Tipper."

Tipper stood, reached for her coat, almost dropped it, managed to get hold of it and put it over her arm.

She took a deep breath and on the exhale wished her minister a blessed day as well, and left.

In her car, Tipper lit a cigarette with slightly trembling hands, took a deep drag, inhaled, and held the smoke for several seconds before exhaling.

"What in hell is going on? Having those kids really changed her, and not for the better. She used to be so mousy."

She got her cellphone out of her purse and told it to call Mary Lou.

# 36

## MONDAY, JANUARY 13, 9:17 AM

THE NINERS, my name for the coffee klatch group that gathers every morning at nine here at the Really Good, were sitting around the tables drinking coffee, eating pastries, and swapping gossip and stories.

When there was a lull in the lies and half-truths being shared, Graham Huston said, "Full moon tonight."

That was all he said. His face was a complete deadpan.

Chief Jager's eyes narrowed slightly. "You taking up astronomy, Huston?"

"Not especially. No news in it. On the other hand, we human beings have a morbid interest in death and dead people."

"You're right about that," the Presbyterian minister, Billy Bob Baskin, said.

Graham continued. "Any way to stop number eight from happening tonight?"

"Don't have a clue as to what you're getting at, Huston," the police chief said.

"The Full Moon Murderer," Magnolia Nadine said. (She's president of the Junior Service League, and a force to be reckoned with.)

Jager stood. "Thanks for the coffee and doughnuts, Harry. Gotta run. Duty calls."

And the police chief was out the door.

"I don't understand why they don't want to talk about this newest killer," Caroline McCluskey, the town librarian, said. "It's not like we're unaware of the creep's existence."

"And thoughts, Harry?" Graham asked. "You're Sovern's good buddy these days. He tell you anything?"

"I promised I wouldn't say a word."

"Oh, pooh," Magnolia Nadine said. "That's crazy."

I shrugged. "Well, I did. If I betray Reece's confidence, then he won't be talking to me and I'll be on his bad side again. And I'm tired of being there."

"Can't blame you for that," Terall Whitacre said. She and her husband, Telford, run T&T Tobacconists. "From everything you've told Telford and me, you've had your share of unwanted attention from those pledged to serve and protect."

"Buck and Tommy can't keep a lid on it forever," Graham said. "Eventually, someone will talk. People can't keep secrets to save their souls."

"Sad, but true," Reverend Baskin said.

A few minutes later, gossip exhausted, the meeting broke up.

Estrelita and I bussed the tables and put them back to their original configuration.

The way I look at it is we'd either have murder number eight tonight, or the killer had already vamoosed for a new pasture.

I grabbed a coffee and another doughnut and sat at my table in the corner. I brought the Crimson Dawn website up on my tablet.

There was nothing about the full moon. Then again, it could be that information wasn't for the general public, or maybe even initiates. Only for the more advanced enlightened. Perhaps the deep inner secrets were only given to those who paid for them.

*And what if money isn't the motive here? Then we have some genuine kooks on our hands — and they will be much more difficult to track down.*

# 37

## MONDAY, JANUARY 13, 11:28 AM

AFTER TIPPER DEPARTED, Ember next saw Waymon Riggins, the chairman of the finance committee, and Euel Pinckney, the church treasurer, at the same time. After all, they both dealt with money. The three discussed options on what to spend the three hundred thousand dollar budget surplus.

Ember wanted to hire a pastor for seniors. When Pinckney said they had the Reverend Humphrey, Ember told the men that it was likely the bishop would be reassigning him.

The two men spluttered, but didn't say much.

As for the surplus, both were inclined to keep the money in the bank for a rainy day.

Ember decided she wasn't going to get anywhere with the men. They would take, no matter what, a position opposing hers.

*This will have to go before the church council,* she told herself, and wished the men a good day.

She was waiting for Claiborne Allen, the council chairperson, when there was a commotion in the outer office, and then Mary Lou Fight stormed into Ember's office.

With cane in hand, Mary Lou brought it down on Ember's desk with a loud thwack.

Instinctively, Ember's hand shot out and wrenched the stick out of Mary Lou's grasp.

She stood and said, her voice a low growl, "Don't you ever do that again, Mrs. Fight. You may think otherwise, but I am the servant of the Lord and in His house you will reverence Him with proper decorum. Otherwise, remember Elisha and those who taunted him."

"You petty, nasty little strumpet. You will call the bishop and rescind your request to transfer Reverend Humphrey."

Ember sat and lay the cane across her desk, leaving one hand on it.

"Please sit, Mrs. Fight."

"I will not. You will do as I say. Pick up the phone and dial the bishop's number."

"I will not."

"Very well. If that is how you wish to play it. You, my little pretty, are doomed."

"I knew this day was coming. So I was prepared." Ember pointed with the cane. "There and there. Cameras to record your actions. Attached to the front of the desk is a microphone. There is also one there and there. You, Mrs. Fight, are on Candid Camera."

Ember didn't smile, but she was pleased to see the old woman blanch for a moment.

Mary Lou took a deep breath. "Please give me back my walking stick."

Ember stood. "Thank you for stopping by. You do remember I'm friends with Graham Huston and his columnist, Monika Crow? Of course you do. You know most things. But not all things. Here's your cane. Have a blessed day, Mrs. Fight. As always, I pray for you."

Mary Lou took the stick and retreated from the office. Rather regally, Ember thought.

She sat. *One of us just jumped from the frying pan into the fire.*

# 38

## MONDAY, JANUARY 13, 1:48 PM

Mary Lou Fight was beside herself. She'd called the bishop's office six times since leaving Reverend Cole's office. Each time she was told, the bishop was not available. She couldn't understand it. He'd *always* answered her calls.

She was stymied and she was furious. The strumpet had completely outplayed her. And was now making threats to her!

"It is clear," she murmured, "the lounge lizard has bought not only my church, but the bishop too. Well, two can play that game."

After all, Mary Lou reasoned, she had money. If all it took was money, then she'd beat the lounge lizard at his own game. Her need for a seat on the church council was now obvious. It was time to step out of the shadows. Time she got behind the wheel herself, so to speak.

"I can see I've greatly underestimated you, my pretty," she said to herself. "But no longer. Now the gloves come off, as they say."

The Reverend Adelbert Humphrey the fourth parked his metallic purple Lexus in front of the parsonage. Right behind the old beat up dingy white van. He got out of his car, looked at the eyesore, and read the faded letters.

Ace Heating and Plumbing

He wondered which of his neighbors was having a heating or plumbing problem. No one was in the vehicle, otherwise he would have told them to move the eyesore and park in a different location.

Retrieving the grocery bag from the passenger side of his car, he walked up the walk and let himself in.

He set the bag containing his Piggly-Wiggly deli lunch on the dining room table and continued on to the kitchen to retrieve his corkscrew.

Returning to the dining room, he screamed, and the corkscrew fell from his hand.

For sitting at his table were two men and a woman.

"Who are you? Where did you come from? What do you want?"

The woman said, "You."

Humphrey turned and ran to the back door. He didn't make it. One of his unwanted guests tackled him and threw him to the floor five feet from freedom.

Adelbert started screaming for help until something hard hit his right ear, and then he began whimpering until the duct tape silenced his mouth.

---

Reece Sovern ended the call with GJ. The picture she'd given him of Kari Lynn Waskowski, while not much different from the one given him by her brother, was nevertheless puzzling.

Twenty-nine. Joined the army right out of high school. Served three years as a clerk in a maintenance battalion headquarters unit. No college. No Vo-Tec. Didn't have many friends. Worked as a stocker at Tischler's and spent her non-work hours playing video games, both online and on her thirty-two inch TV.

She had a thousand bucks in her checking account and sixty-seven hundred in her savings account. GJ got that information from her recent bank statement.

Reece chuckled. "Old-fashioned. Like me. Got paper statements."

No will. At least she'd never mentioned having one to anyone.

First started corresponding with the countesses two years ago. Then joined the New Order of the Crimson Dawn nine months later.

Dues were a hundred bucks a month. That information was in an email. But it didn't say where the money was sent.

A year ago, she was invited to attend a full moon service in Long Needle, Louisiana. She explained to the countesses she couldn't get off work to attend.

Then she got a second invite to attend the December full moon service in Magnolia Bluff.

"And we know what happened at that service," Reece said to himself.

He hoped they got the warrant for the bank accounts soon. *Be helpful to know where that dues money was sent.*

He leaned back in his chair. *Tonight's another full moon.*

And even though Reece wasn't a praying man, he said a prayer.

## 39

### MONDAY, JANUARY 13, 2:01 PM

THE RESERVOIR WAS QUIET. The cool day, a high of only 57 degrees Fahrenheit, was keeping the boaters at home.

Scarlett Hayden let her Sundancer 370 cabin cruiser drift with the current while she reclined on the built-in bench seat, sipping her martini.

She'd been seeing Harry's lawyer, Stanton Mirabeau Lauderbach, for some time now in an attempt to move on. But as nice as Stanton was, he wasn't Harry Thurgood, and therein lay the problem.

If there was no Harry Thurgood, Stanton would be her man, heart and soul. He was attentive and made her feel good.

"But Harry Thurgood is alive and well," she told her martini glass, and proceeded to down a third of the piney liquid.

She'd killed two men to protect him from Mary Lou Fight, only to watch him slip away to the arms of Ember Cole. Only Dr. Mike Kurelek was privy to her dark secret. And for all the time she'd spent in therapy with him, she still wanted Harry more than anything else in the world.

"And now he has those damn kids. I'll never get him away from her." She swallowed another third of her drink.

Kurelek had asked her why Harry Thurgood. She'd told him

how one day, looking in the mirror before taking her shower, she realized a day would come, and probably soon, when the football players wouldn't want to dance with the old white ho any longer. And before that day came, she wanted a man with whom to share the rest of her life.

"So why Harry?" Kurelek had pressed.

"He has money. He has style. He has grace. He's intelligent. And he makes me laugh."

"And Stanton doesn't?" Kurelek had said.

"Oh, he does," Scarlett told him. "Just not in the same measure as Harry."

And for Scarlett, therein lay the rub. It was the difference between a Chevy and a Cadillac.

She finished her drink, got up and made herself a new one, and returned to her seat.

The boat drifted, and Scarlett drank.

After a time, a thought occurred to her. With all the murders Magnolia Bluff was experiencing, who would notice one more?

*One more death probably wouldn't matter overly much,* she told herself.

And if it didn't much matter, perhaps the answer to her problem was giving Ember Cole eternal rest at the bottom of the reservoir.

## 40

### MONDAY, JANUARY 13, 2:05 PM

THE WARRANT CAME through and Reece got Kari Waskowski's bank information for the past two years.

He scanned the printout and when finished, tossed it on his desk, muttering a colorful word worthy of a former Marine.

"PayPal. She used PayPal to pay that bunch of nutters. Now we're back to the cyber investigation. Damn. Damn. And double damn."

He took a deep breath, pushed his glasses up, exhaled, and took a cigar out of his desk drawer. Cellophane removed, he stuck it in the left corner of his mouth and held it there between his teeth and cheek.

*Okay,* he told himself, *there's a group of nutters around here killing people on the night of the full moon. The murders started in June near as we can determine. So why June? Why start then?*

Reece chewed on his cigar and chewed on his question. After a time, he concluded that the killer probably didn't live in the county or Magnolia Bluff much before June.

*Say the killer moves here a month or two, maybe three, before the first killing. That would account for the first death in June. After all, it would take the killer some time to get settled and start working on convincing people to come here.*

Reece leaned forward and looked through his notes.

*A year ago, they'd invited Kari Waskowski to attend the full moon shindig in Louisiana. Which means sometime between January and June last year our perp moves to our county.*

He smiled. "I guess I'd best start talking to real estate agents."

---

The Reverend Ember Cole had no interviews scheduled for the afternoon. She'd taken a trip home to nurse the twins, then headed to the police station to tell Reece her idea to check on the new people who'd moved to the area. She ran into him just as he was leaving the station.

"Hello, Reece."

"Well, Reverend, good afternoon."

"And a good afternoon to you as well. You know, you can call me Ember."

"Well, uh, thank you. Although it's a bit difficult for me to get beyond that collar and cross you're wearing."

"That's okay. Just keep in mind that you can call me Ember."

"Okay, Reverend, uh, Ember, I'll keep that in mind."

"Do you have a minute? I have an idea I'd like to share with you."

"Sure. Walk with me to my car. So what's your idea?"

"Since this current string of murders started in June, I'm thinking there's a good chance the killer or killers moved here sometime before then. So if you checked with the realtors in the area to get a list of who moved here, say from January to May of last year, you might find the killer in that group."

Reece chuckled. "Well, uh, Ember, I guess great minds think alike. I just came to the same conclusion myself."

"Really? That's great."

"Thanks for sharing your idea. I appreciate it."

They reached Reece's car.

"Can I give you a lift?"

"No, that's all right. My car is at the church. I'll walk."

"Hop in. It'll give us a couple more minutes to talk."

"Okay."

Ember got into the front passenger seat as Reece slid behind the wheel.

"It's a different experience sitting up here."

"Yeah. I'm—"

"Shush. Bygones are bygones, Reece. Okay?"

"Okay. Thanks. So, uh, when did you come up with this idea?"

He started the car, reversed, and drove out of the lot.

"Last night talking with Harry."

"I guess you had the jump on me then. Let me level with you. I don't care what Briggs says. Over the past few years, we've gotten a lot of valuable intel from all you folks. Sometimes it's a bit humiliating to have y'all showin' up the department, but you and Harry have been really good about it. Unlike some jerks around here."

Ember laughed. "Brandon is a pretty good guy, you know."

"I suppose he is. He's a cop after all. We got off on the wrong foot and I don't ever see us getting on the right foot."

"It's worth a try, isn't it?"

"Maybe he should."

"Perhaps you're right. But you can't control him. You can only control you."

"Wise words, Parson. We're here. Thanks for the tip. I appreciate it."

"My pleasure. Let us know if we can help."

"I will."

"Thanks, Reece. Bye."

Ember exited the car and watched him drive off.

*Reece is a decent guy underneath that rough exterior. Hopefully, he and Brandon will work things out. And while he lacks imagination, I think he's growing. Learning to look outside of his box. He'll get these baddies. I know he will.*

## 41

MONDAY, JANUARY 13, 6:02 PM

RATHER THAN LET Graham Huston eat his to-go supper alone, I invited him to have supper with Em and I. He was reluctant at first, but finally gave in.

We drove in my car to the former rail baron mansion that's now my home.

Princess greeted us at the door, sniffed Graham and gave her approval.

"Pretty pup," he said. "What breed did you say she is?"

"A Hovawart. A recreation of the medieval German castle defense dog. They're not attack dogs, but they will defend you with their lives."

"Huh. Learn something new every day."

We made our way to the family room. Em was there. I gave her a kiss and she and Graham exchanged hellos. Graham sat on one of the loveseats.

"What'll you have to drink?" I asked him.

"Have any Blue Corn Bourbon?"

"Sure do. Just for you."

"Two fingers. Neat."

"You want anything, Em?"

"How about club soda with lime?"

I poured and squeezed and handed Graham and Em their libations. For myself, I mixed a green Chartreuse with water to reduce the alcohol.

Graham took a sip of his bourbon. "What are the odds murder number eight will happen tonight?"

"Oh, Graham, you would," Ember said. "You'll ruin supper."

"I have a paper to put out. And in spite of the gag order, people are asking questions. They're starting to fear they might be next. They want answers. And I don't want to tell them fiction."

"Not sure your readers are going to get answers, at least from any official source, unless someone is willing to speak off the record," I said.

"And no one, thus far, is willing to take that risk." He took a sip of whiskey. "What about this cult? The New Order of the Crimson Dawn. Have you heard anything about it, Ember? Or any of your cohorts?"

"No one in the ministerial association has said anything."

"They might not, but that doesn't mean some of their members, particularly the younger members or lonely members, aren't involved."

"True." Em dragged out the word, as though reluctantly admitting Graham's point.

"What about your church?"

"No one has come to me asking my opinion about the cult."

"I find it odd that we've had these nut jobs in our midst for over half a year, it could even be longer, and no one has said anything. No one has a friend or relative involved in the group?"

"Since it's online, it's possible they get very little, if any, local traffic," I said. "In this day and age, the world is your audience."

"You do have a point there." Graham took a swallow of bourbon. "It's just mighty odd, if you ask me."

"It is that," I agreed. "But if they pick and choose the victims, inviting them to a rural location, and stay on the move, they are going to be difficult to catch. Unless we find out who's behind the curtain."

Graham finished his drink. "Which means we are at the mercy of the Rangers it seems at this point."

"Aren't they supposed to be better than the FBI?" Em asked.

"That's what they like to say," Graham said.

"I think our supper is calling," I said.

"Good. I'm starved," our newspaperman declared.

We left the family room and made our way to the dining room.

I asked Em what Jerri made for us.

She said, "Pork chops with tomato gravy, mashed potatoes, biscuits, peas with bacon, and brown butter sweet potato pie."

"Man," Graham said. "Can't you two walk faster?"

---

After we'd polished off the victuals, we took our second cups of coffee to the family room.

I stoked up the fire while Graham returned the discussion to the cult group.

"What are your thoughts on a *Chronicle* article concerning the group and requesting local members to contact me?"

I shrugged. "You might get a bite."

"It's worth a try," Em said.

Graham drained his coffee cup. "If you don't mind, Harry, giving me a lift to the office? I got an article to write and a paper to finish putting together."

I drank my coffee and told him not a problem.

As I drove to the *Chronicle* office, I asked him, "Are you sure it's wise to stir the pot? This group of nutters are killers."

Graham paused briefly before responding. "It's true someone in the group is a killer. My guess is that it's someone high up. And they aren't likely to respond."

"For your sake, my friend, I hope you're right."

# 42

## MONDAY, JANUARY 13, 11:08 PM

FOUR METAL FIRE pits illuminated the barn. They sat outside the circle of thirteen men and women holding hands and chanting in Greek. All but two wore crimson robes.

Inside the circle was a rectangular wooden platform.

On the platform was a naked woman. Her wrists and ankles were tied to stakes that had been hammered into the thick wooden floor boards.

Her eyes were half closed, and she muttered, "Eternal life from eternal death."

At a signal from one of the two white-robed women standing behind the head of the bound woman, the chanting stopped. She withdrew from a sheath belted to her waist a black obsidian knife and said, "Eternal life from eternal death."

The other white-robed woman pulled her black obsidian knife from its sheath and said, "We vrykolakos take life from life and live forever. May this acolyte join us as her reward for giving us eternal life."

She stepped forward, lay the knife between the breasts of the woman on the platform. Taking a ball gag from a pocket in her robe, she put it in the naked woman's mouth, slipped the strap over her head, and tightened it. She kissed the woman's cheeks, picked up the knife, found a vein in her left arm, and slashed the vein halfway up the woman's arm.

A muffled scream rent the air.

The white-robed woman made sure the blood flowed into a glass container.

The other woman in white stepped forward, kissed the bound and gagged woman on each cheek, and walked down to her right leg.

She said, "From this body, we drink and eat and live forever. Eternal life from eternal death."

Then she slashed deep into the leg near the sacrifice's groin and was rewarded with a geyser of blood and a muffled scream.

The woman in white, who was standing on the left side of the dying woman, walked to the right and in less than half a minute she'd cut open the victim's abdomen and extracted her liver.

One of them said, "This is the flesh that gives us life. Drink and eat of this body and live forever. Sister Davorka, please distribute the blood. Sister Goody, please distribute the liver."

Sister Davorka picked up the bowl of blood and made her way around the circle letting each worshipper drink.

Sister Goody picked up skewers and put a piece of liver on each one as it was cut off. When all the skewers contained a piece of meat, one was given to each of the worshippers.

Some ate the liver raw, others roasted it over the fires in the fire pits.

When everyone had a piece of liver, the white-robed women cut off pieces of the organ for themselves and fed each other.

After eating and drinking, one of the white robes walked around the circle, smeared blood on each person, and commanded him or her to love the neighbor to their left.

After this, the two women clothed in white discarded their robes, smeared blood on each other, went to the woman who had no partner, and joined the orgy.

# 43

## TUESDAY, JANUARY 14, 6:32 AM

Reece Sovern and GJ Riggins sat in his office drinking coffee and eating doughnuts.

"Good to have you back," Reece said, before tucking into his raised glazed doughnut.

"Good to be back, Sarge." She took a sip of coffee and then bit into her chocolate covered Bismarck.

"I asked Briggs to pass the word that every officer needs to be extra vigilant. If there was a murder, and the killer dumped the body in our jurisdiction, we want to find it ASAP."

"Is the sheriff doing the same?"

"I believe so. Although they have more territory to cover."

GJ nodded. "And lots more out-of-the-way places."

"Right. We're going to spend today searching the city, right along with everyone else."

"Should I take my car?"

"No. We'll go together. I want you to fill me in on everything you discovered in Chicago."

"Should we go now?"

"Let's finish our coffee first."

Reece's desk phone rang. He picked it up. "Sovern."

"Reece, this is Harry Thurgood."

"Morning Harry. What can I do for you?"

"Well, I think you'd best come out to my place. My dog found something you'll want to see."

Reece felt a tingling in his spine. "Okay, I'm on my way."

He hung up and looked at GJ. "Thurgood. His dog found something he thinks we need to see."

"A body?"

"He didn't say. But that's what I'm thinking. Grab your coffee and let's go."

---

Reece lost no time in getting to my place. I left Princess in the house and walked out to his car.

"Good morning Reece, GJ."

Reece and I shook hands. GJ gave me a nod, and I gave her a big smile in return.

I don't think she cares much for me or Em. But that's her problem. To me, she's just another person on the planet. And I try to treat everyone the same.

In spite of all the stories about her hitting on guys, I have a feeling, based on nothing but casual observation, she doesn't actually like men all that much. Which I find somewhat amusing as she dresses like a man and wears her hair like one, too. Then again, that might be her attempt to be just one of the guys. In any event, it's her life and she's welcome to it. Just another example of all the different ways our species rolls.

"So, what do you have for us?" Reece asked.

"Follow me."

My home sits on five acres, so it was a fair walk to the back forty, as I call it.

"I was walking Princess, oh, about half an hour before I called. She's still a pup, so I wanted to make sure she didn't wander too far."

"Yeah, pups will do that. Have to be taught the boundaries," Reece said.

"Right. So we were out walking, when suddenly her nose lifted, and she went on alert. I said to her, 'What is it?' She started whining, and I said, 'Show me.' And off she ran. I trotted after her."

"Was it a body?" GJ asked.

"Yes, it was. And I'm guessing it's last night's victim."

"So why on your property?" GJ asked. Suspicion laced her voice.

"Can't rightly say. But here we are. You tell me."

She uttered an expletive. Reece took a cigar out of his pocket, removed the cellophane, and sank his teeth into it. He pushed his glasses up and shook his head.

"I suppose you'll be sending for the entire crew, eh?"

"You got that right," he said.

I smiled. "Lucky for you, the Full Moon Killer made a mistake."

Reece walked around the body, stooped down to scrutinize it, and finally stood up.

"No, Harry," he said, "not my lucky day. I'm convinced this is the work of a copycat."

# 44

## TUESDAY, JANUARY 14, 7:48 AM

ASIDE FROM REECE AND GJ, there was the MBPD photographer, the ambulance crew, MBPD officers Logan Ytzen and Dick Schreiber, MBPD sergeant Andrew LaPorte, four deputies from the Burnet County Sheriff's department, and Captain Briggs.

True to form, Briggs showed up right after Ytzen and Schreiber arrived and immediately got in my face.

"What are you doing here, Thurgood? This is a crime scene, and *you* aren't one of my officers."

"Well, Captain, I'm the landowner here and I'm the one who reported the body."

"Good. Now, you go stand over there and wait for someone to take your statement. Then you can leave."

"Uh, this is my land. I'm not leaving."

"Do you want me to arrest you for obstructing justice?"

"Do you want Stanton Lauderbach to teach you the definition of obstructing justice?"

"Look here, Thurgood—"

"No, you look here, Briggs. Do you want to be slapped with another harassment suit?"

"I'm not harassing you."

"And I'm not obstructing justice, either."

I stared at him, and he stared at me. And we stayed that way, playing chicken, seeing who'd blink first. In the end, Em interrupted our showdown.

"What's going on, Harry? Why are the police and deputies here?"

"Sorry for not telling you," I said. "I thought Reece should know first. Princess found a body."

"Oh, no. Here we go again."

"What's that mean?" Briggs asked.

Em put her fists on her hips. "We're going to be harassed by you people again."

"Now look here, Mrs. Thurgood."

"I'm Ms. Cole or Reverend Cole, Captain."

"Oh, uh, sorry."

Em ignored Briggs and asked me, "Do you know who was killed?"

"The body is mutilated, but it seems to me there's something familiar about it."

"Maybe I should take a look," Em said.

Briggs cleared his throat. "Rather gruesome, ma'am."

"After seeing Cally's body, I think I can stomach anything."

Briggs shrugged. "Okay. Follow me."

We followed him to where the body still lay.

One look and Em put her hand to her mouth, stepped back, and fell to her knees.

I dropped to my knees and put my arms around her.

She choked back a sob. "Oh, Harry, this is bad. That's Adelbert."

# 45

## TUESDAY, JANUARY 14, 9:13 AM

Briggs's response to Ember's declaration was to pack us off in separate vehicles to the police station. I was able to get a text off to Lauderbach and he was waiting for us when we showed up at the MBPD station.

Em was put in Interrogation Room One and I in Room Two. And since they were waiting for female officers to question her, Lauderbach was with me. He was leaning back in his chair with his hands behind his head.

Our good cop, bad cop duo was Reece and Briggs.

Reece started. "Did you recognize the victim when your dog found him, Harry?"

"No. Although I thought he looked familiar. But when a guy's had his man parts shoved into his mouth, has a gaping hole where his liver should be, and multiple stab wounds, he does look different from if he was, say, wearing a suit."

"You think this funny, Thurgood?" Briggs said.

"No. I was just saying."

"Did you know the Reverend Humphrey?" Reece asked.

"Not really. We didn't socialize. I knew who he was, and that was it."

"Why didn't you socialize with him?" Briggs asked. "He was the assistant minister at your church."

"Yes, he was. That doesn't mean we were bosom buddies. I saw him at Sunday worship and once or twice at a church council meeting. Otherwise, he didn't exist. So to speak."

"Why is his body on your land?" Briggs asked.

"It seems to me, Captain, you'll need to ask who killed him to get the answer to that question."

"It's awfully suspicious, Thurgood, that the body was left on your land."

"How so?"

He leaned back in his chair and crossed his arms over his chest. "Well, there was that secretary who killed someone. Then your involvement with the traveling evangelist. And the parishioner who brutally butchered her mother and four other people, and afterwards blew up herself and her father. Now this. Kind of a dangerous church to be a member of. Don't you think? Or maybe it's just you and your wife."

I lifted my shoulders and let them drop, making an exaggerated shrug. "Well, Captain, perhaps it has nothing to do with myself and my wife. Maybe it's karma for a church that accepts someone like Mary Lou Fight as a member there."

"Or maybe this has something to do with what you're not telling us about your secret life. Maybe it's Mafia retribution or something."

Lauderbach stepped in. "And how is this relevant, Mr. Briggs? Perhaps you should stick to this murder and the facts, and quit the speculation. Hm? After all, you wouldn't want a suit brought against you for defamation of character, now would you?"

Reece asked, "How often do you go to that area of your property?"

"It varies. That section? I don't know. Two or three times in the month?"

"What about mowing?" Briggs asked.

"I have a lawn service."

The captain snorted. "Of course you do."

I ignored the jab. "Five acres is a good size chunk of land. I probably check out the entire acreage in the course of a month. I am quite busy with the coffee shop, you know."

Briggs snorted, but said nothing.

Reece cast a glance towards his boss, pushed his glasses up, and said, "So it was a bit of luck your dog found the body while it was fresh."

"I guess I'd say you're right."

Reece continued. "So, who would want the church's assistant pastor dead?"

"I don't have a clue. Em said the old people loved him. Not knowing him, I have no idea if he had enemies who'd resort to murder."

"What has your wife said?" Briggs asked.

"You'll have to ask her."

The captain pressed on. "So there's nothing you can tell us. Is that what you're saying?"

"I believe I've told you all I know. Now, if something comes to mind later, I'll let you know."

Reece said, "After the ME does the autopsy, we may have additional questions. In the meantime, we'd prefer it if you didn't leave the county."

"So I'm free to go?"

"You are," Reece said.

"Quite an improvement on the past."

"Don't get cocky, Thurgood," Briggs said. "You're a material witness and—"

Lauderbach cut him off. "You know, Captain, here in Magnolia Bluff honey works better than vinegar. Something you need to keep in mind."

"You telling me how to do my job?"

Lauderbach favored Briggs with a big smile. "Just a little friendly advice from an insider to an outsider."

I added, "It'll pay you in spades to heed it."

Briggs shook his head. "Wise guy. Get outta here."

# 46

## TUESDAY, JANUARY 14, 10:08 AM

STANTON LAUDERBACH PATTED Ember Cole's shoulder. "Don't worry, Ember. Just answer their questions. I'll jump in if they get off course. Okay?"

"Just like before."

"Exactly."

"I wonder who the bloodhounds will be today?"

Stanton laughed. "Don't know. Don't care. I'm the best lawyer in the county, and probably the state."

Ember smiled. "I appreciate your confidence."

"Confidence is a mental attitude. And mine is based on fact. Not wishful thinking."

The door opened and in walked two women with blonde hair. Ember recognized the one. Officer Georgia Jean Riggins. She didn't recognize the other woman.

Stanton stood. "Ms. Riggins. Ms. Horton."

The women sat, and Stanton returned to his seat.

He turned to Ember. "I believe you know Officer Riggins. Amanda Horton is an Assistant District Attorney."

Ember said, "Hello," and the Assistant DA replied with a tight smile.

Stanton said, "And how are you ladies doing this fine morning?"

Horton replied, "As well as can be expected. Shall we get on with it? I have a busy schedule today."

"By all means," Stanton replied.

Georgia Jean fired the opening salvo. "Let's see… Your church secretary, then the lay leader of your church, and now your assistant pastor. Where were you from, say, six-thirty yesterday evening to when your husband discovered the body this morning?"

Ember said a silent prayer, took a moment to compose her thoughts, then said, "I was at home."

"Took you long enough to come up with that answer. Lose your place in the script?"

Ember stood. "Do you have something you want to say, Officer? I'm getting sick and tired of your attitude."

Stanton touched her arm. When she looked at him, she caught the almost imperceptible shake of his head.

Ember took a deep breath and sat.

Stanton said, "We are on a fact finding mission, Ms. Riggins. Perhaps it would be best if you saved the vinegar for another time."

Amanda Horton took over. "You were at home. Anyone with you?"

"My husband and the nanny. Our housekeeper and cook had already left for the day."

"No one else?"

"The children. But they aren't old enough to help us kill people."

Stanton barely suppressed a smile.

The Assistant DA gave Ember the squint eye.

GJ said, "What did you say? This isn't a joke, Reverend."

"I didn't say it was," Ember replied. "But you are treating me like a criminal, and I resent it."

GJ was about to reply, but a touch on her arm stopped her.

Horton clarified, "So, your husband, children, and their nanny were with you from six-thirty until this morning when your husband found the body."

"That's correct."

"Do you have any idea why someone would want to kill..." She looked at her notes. "Reverend Humphrey?"

"No, I do not. He was very popular with the senior women in the church. He will be missed."

"He had no enemies?" GJ asked.

"I can't say if he had enemies or not. There were some people at the church who didn't care for him overly much."

"Why?" GJ asked.

"Internal church politics. Just like some people don't care overly much for me. But an actual enemy? Someone who wanted him dead? At Saint Luke's? No, I can't think of anyone with that degree of animosity. And outside of the church, I wouldn't have any idea."

Horton said, "So you have no notion as to why he was so brutally murdered?"

"No, I don't. It is a mystery. He hasn't been with us all that long. It has to be someone he knew before coming to Saint Luke's."

"What was your opinion of him?" GJ asked.

"I thought he was an officious prig. But the senior women loved him, so he was of value to the ministry at the church."

"Isn't that a put down?" Horton asked.

"I didn't like him. He was full of himself. But he was useful. His presence allowed me to do what I wanted to do."

"And that was?" GJ asked.

"Minister to the young people who need Jesus."

Assistant District Attorney Horton stood. "That's all for now. We may have more questions after the autopsy, so we'd appreciate it if you didn't leave the county without notifying us."

Ember and Stanton stood. He said, "Have a good day, ladies." He then guided Ember to the door, and they left.

"You were rather bristly in there today," he said.

"I'm sick and tired of Officer Riggins and her nasty attitude."

"I can understand that. Next time, though, it might help if you turned the other cheek. She wants to tick you off. Don't give her the pleasure."

"All right. The other cheek it is. Thanks, Stanton."

"My pleasure, Ember. Now, to find out what the grapevine has heard."

# 47

## TUESDAY, JANUARY 14, 11:38 AM

After our interviews, maybe interrogations would be a better descriptor, Em and I stopped at the Really Good for something to eat.

Eight customers were in the shop, which surprised me. One was Reece Sovern, another was Graham Huston.

To Em, I whispered, "We're popular today."

She responded, resignation in her voice, "Why does it always have to be a murder?"

"Price of fame, I guess."

"Well, Mister, we should get ourselves a couple of chainsaws and really give them something to talk about."

I let out a laugh. "Not a guarantee for flying under the radar."

"Would be colorful, though."

"That it would."

We walked up to Reece.

"You got here fast," I said. "Official, or unofficial?"

With a smirk on his face, he answered, "Unofficially official."

"This will be good," I said. "Head over to my table. I'm going to corral Graham."

Em went with Reece while I grabbed our newspaperman. On the way, I signaled to Estrelita and pointed to my table.

When we'd all sat down, she showed up to take our orders.

"And before you two balk," I began, "lunch is on me."

"It's no wonder you don't make any money," Graham said.

"Says who?" I responded.

"Half the town."

And Reece added, "The other half think it, even if they don't say it."

I lifted my shoulders an inch and let them down again. "I'm still in business."

"And that's the source for some very fanciful rumors," Graham said.

"I'm sure. Fanciful rumors aside, order whatever you want."

"Harry does okay here," Ember said.

Graham, without giving it a second thought, looked at Estrelita and said, "Chili, corn bread, water."

"I'll have the chicken noodle soup, biscuits and gravy, and a Dr. Pepper," Reece said.

Ember ordered soup and a salad, and I ordered two BLTs on white with a coffee and cream.

Estrelita left, and I asked Reece what it was he wanted to talk about.

"Rather than go to every realtor in the county, I called the County Clerk's Office and the Burnet Central Appraisal District Office and asked them to send me what they had on property changes and appraisals since the first of last year. Probably get the information next decade. Overworked and understaffed, like all of us."

"Maybe we can help," Graham said.

"Briggs would love that," Ember said.

Reece nodded, "Yeah, he would."

Estrelita brought our food and left. The conversation paused while we got ourselves settled for the midday feed.

Once settled, Graham picked up the conversation. "I'm serious. I can assign Monika, Rob Carter, Landon Pace, and possibly Tom Hedrick, if he can get away from his tire store."

Reece swallowed a spoonful of soup. "Doesn't Hedrick just do sports?"

"So far. But if he isn't too busy with his store, he might be able to fly under the radar better than the others."

"Got a point there, Huston." Reece drank Dr. Pepper. "In fact, who'd question y'all stoppin' by the Appraisal Office or the Clerk's Office?"

"Anyone can do so," Ember said.

"Right you are, Reverend." Reece spooned more soup. "Let me see how many I can put on it before y'all start playing super sleuth. While we can probably slip this past Briggs, I don't want y'all running into someone official and word getting back to him."

"Understandable. Just give us the nod if we can be of help," I said.

"Oh, I will," Reece replied. "Don't you worry about that."

Graham finished his bowl of chili. "What can you tell me about the newest murder in town?"

Reece chuckled. "I can tell you the person's dead."

"C'mon, Reece, you know that...," he looked at his watch, "in another hour, over half the town will know about the murder. And there will be all manner of speculation. Monika's already heard...," Graham's eyes shifted to Ember, "that the victim was the assistant pastor at Ember's church."

Reece leaned back in his chair. "Oh, she has, has she?"

"You forget, Monika's a hometown girl. She got the information from her aunt, who got it from her friend, whose granddaughter works at the hospital and knows the ambulance driver, who's friends with Mary Lou Fight's maid."

"What a tangled web," Reece said.

Graham pressed on. "Info from an anonymous source?"

"Why do you need me?" Reece asked. "You have half the town."

"Very true. But I'm putting out a special edition tomorrow, and I'd like something that at least smells official."

"Best talk to Briggs."

"Tried. He barely hinted he was even aware I existed."

"I'd say he probably made a mistake there."

"Probably. I have some pretty large typeface I'm just dying to use."

"Okay, Huston. We'll talk, but somewhere less public. I'll swing by your office later. Well, folks, I'd best be going. Harry, can I get a doggie bag for my biscuits and gravy?"

I signaled Estrelita, gave her the doggie bag sign, and pointed to Reece.

"Sure would like to know how you do that," Reece said.

"Do what?" I asked.

"Control people so effortlessly."

"More like the conductor of a symphony. Just guiding well-rehearsed performers."

Estrelita arrived, transferred Reece's food to the box, put it in a bag, and gave it to him.

When she left, Reece stood. "I don't believe it."

Graham laughed. "The secret is he's conducting *well-paid* performers."

I laughed.

Reece nodded. "Yeah. Probably more like it."

He left, and I said to Graham, "Special edition, eh?"

"Yep. The people are getting scared. They want to know what's going on." He looked over at Em. "The victim was your assistant pastor, wasn't it?"

"Yes. But you didn't hear that from me."

"Of course not." His eyes took both of us in. "Full Moon Killer victim?"

I shook my head. "But you didn't get that from me."

"Of course not. Well, you two, I suppose our sergeant investigator wants that kept under the rug."

"For now," I said. "Not sure how the gendarmes are going to play it. But for now, they want it kept quiet."

Graham shook his head. "That will only work until someone figures out the truth and sparks a stampede."

# 48

## TUESDAY, JANUARY 14, 1:24 PM

AFTER OUR LUNCH, I dropped Em off at home to nurse the twins. With her and the babes doing their thing, I returned to the Really Good. After she fed the twins, Em planned to spend some time at the church.

I parked in the alley behind the shop and entered through the back door. Crossing through the kitchen, I greeted Miguel. He was putting together a hamburger.

As I walked into the customer area, Jack gave me a lazy salute, Estrelita smiled, and I gave a nod to both.

Grabbing a coffee and a couple of doughnuts, I took up my usual spot at my table in the corner.

My eyes lingered a moment on the people seated in my establishment. Two guys sat at the counter. One had coffee and a slice of pie. Pecan, I think. The other fellow was working on a burger.

Two women, who I recognized as locals, occupied a table.

The only other customer was a fellow I didn't recognize. He was sitting at a table near the big front window nursing a cup of java. Estrelita brought him a hamburger.

I took a sip of coffee and then bit into my doughnut.

The bell over the door rang, and my eyes shifted to see who'd entered. The person was Augustinia Faber.

She smiled at me. I rose and walked over to her.

"Well, Mrs. Faber, what a pleasure."

She held out her hand. I took it in mine and bowed over it.

Her response was a giggle. "You are so fun."

"Join me?"

"I came to get lunch for Mrs. Galt and myself."

"Join me and we can talk while you wait."

I signaled for Estrelita. We sat, and when my waitress arrived, Augustinia gave her the orders.

"Did you get the books?" I asked.

"Yes, we did. A courier service is bringing them to us. We should get them by the end of the week." She paused for a moment before saying, "I sense you are not a man of the church."

"No, I'm not."

"Yet you are married to a minister."

"I am."

"How does that work? It seems so unworkable."

My response was a short laugh. "All I can say is that we're both tolerant, at least sufficiently tolerant, of the other person to not trip over the beliefs we don't agree with."

"That's nice. Your practical approach should provide a stable home for your children."

"That's the plan."

Estrelita set two bags on the table. Augustinia surprised me by giving Estrelita a fifty-dollar bill and telling her to keep the change.

The waitress's eyes widened in surprise. But she recovered quickly, expressed her gratitude and left.

Augustinia stood, and I did too.

"If you are open to the idea, perhaps Mrs. Galt and I will call on you at your home. We want to learn more about you.

"That would be perfectly okay. Perhaps we could have dinner together."

She smiled. "That would be lovely. You are such fascinating people."

She extended her hand. I bowed over it, and she departed.

*Odd woman. Her spouse, too. Wonder why they're interested in Em and me?*

I resumed my seat. *Are they undercover agents?* I chuckled. *I suppose it is possible. Then again, they could just be a lonely people looking for some friends.*

# 49

## TUESDAY, JANUARY 14, 2:25 PM

REECE SOVERN WAS READING through the printout of the ME's report on the late Reverend Adelbert Humphrey a second time. This time making notes in his notebook.

The burning question was whether or not this was the work of the Full Moon Killer.

Reece was pleased to see that the medical examiner felt the answer was no, the same conclusion Reece had come to when he first saw the body.

He noted the differences between the two killers as he read through the report.

When he'd finished, he looked over the short list of differences.

First was the desecration of the body.

*What was the significance of cutting off the man's privates and stuffing them in his mouth?* Reece wondered.

Was the killer telling the minister to F himself?

Or did the killer simply hate men?

Perhaps the minister was a homosexual, and the killer was anti-gay.

Reece pondered on the three possibilities.

If the late Reverend Humphrey was a homosexual, and the

killer hated homosexuals, then that would explain the mutilation.

Reece liked the third option. It made the most sense. He circled it in his notebook.

Second was the instrument used to cut the victims.

According to the ME, the other victims had cuts made with what was probably a very sharp stone knife, the edge created by flaking.

"Perhaps an obsidian knife," the ME had speculated in his report.

The cuts on the minister's body, on the other hand, were made with a stainless steel knife. Somewhat dull. Probably a kitchen knife.

The third difference was the general ignorance of anatomy displayed in the case of the minister.

The killer was unaware of the proper way to cut a vein for maximum blood flow. And he certainly had little understanding on how to remove the liver, let alone find it in the first place.

The exsanguination and the removal of the liver were very clumsily done, according to the ME.

The fourth difference was the disposal of the body.

The Full Moon Killer took great pains to hide the bodies. With the minister, it was as though the killer wanted the body to be found.

Reece rolled the cigar to the other side of his mouth, leaned back in his chair, and gazed at the ceiling.

*Why Thurgood's land? Somebody sending a message to Harry and the Reverend?*

The cigar made its way to the other side of his mouth.

*What is Harry involved in that is such a big secret? And is this murder somehow related to him?*

Reece sat up.

He'd sent GJ out to talk with realtors. That wouldn't help for homes or land sold by owners, or where the realtor was outside of the county. But it was a start, and would have to do until the government offices got back to him. Unless he took Harry, Ember, and Graham up on their offers of assistance.

He didn't want to take GJ off what she was doing.

"Must be someone here who has a bit of free time," he told himself.

He stood and headed for his door.

# 50

## TUESDAY, JANUARY 14, 3:40 PM

Reece walked into the Really Good. He spotted Harry at his table reading an iPad. Also present were a cup of coffee and a couple of doughnuts.

*How the heck does he not get fat from those doughnuts or wired from all that caffeine?*

He studied Harry's three-piece suit, shirt, and tie. Then his eyes drifted down to his own wrinkled sport coat, shirt, and tie. He shook his head. *The man has class. Yes, he does.*

Reece noticed Harry looking at him. He quickly crossed the floor in brisk strides to the coffee man's table.

"Afternoon, Reece."

"Afternoon, Harry."

"Have a seat."

"Thanks."

"Official or unofficial?"

"This visit is official. Want to ask you some questions about Humphrey's murder."

"Okay." He closed the iPad's cover. "Ask away."

Reece took out his notebook and turned to a page. "Why did the man's body end up on your land?"

Harry shrugged. "Don't have a clue."

"Does it have something to do with the Reverend, or the church?"

"My guess — emphasis on *guess* — is that it does have something to do with the church. But I have no idea in relation to what."

"How well did you know him?"

"I didn't. I knew who he was, but I can't recall that we ever had an actual conversation."

"Was he a homosexual?"

Harry smiled. "Now, how would I know that?"

"C'mon, Harry. Indulge me. What are the gossip grannies saying about him?"

"There's talk that perhaps he was. You know, the Liberace thing: he never said, but everyone thought he was. As far as I'm aware, Humphrey never said one way or the other. He may have been, but was not practicing."

Reece nodded. "A celibate gay guy." His eyes shifted a moment to the ceiling, then came back to Harry. "So why the mutilation?"

"A guess, and that's all it is, is that whoever killed him thought he was gay, and the mutilation was some kind of symbolic gesture."

"That kind of mutilation, it would seem to me, screams something sexual."

Harry shrugged. "Your guess is as good as mine."

"I'm still puzzled why the killer would dump the body on your property. I mean, that's telling me it wasn't that the guy was queer, that got him killed, but that he was a homosexual minister. A leader of the church. And *that* got him killed by someone in Ember's church who doesn't like homosexuals."

"Could very well be, Reece, but who that person is, I have no idea. I know of no one who has expressed any anti-gay rhetoric. Not saying there isn't someone, but I don't know that person, or know of him or her."

Reece took a deep breath and exhaled before asking his next

question. "Do you think someone's perhaps sending you a message?"

"If so, I don't know who it is or what the message is."

"The speculation is that you have this secret life or a past you want to keep secret. You know, like Ember."

Harry laughed. "That's the speculation."

"Do you?"

"If I did, and I told you, then it wouldn't be a secret, now, would it?"

Reece chuckled. "No, it wouldn't. But I have to ask, is the body, in its mutilated state, somehow connected with your past, or your present, visible or not visible?"

Harry took a bite of doughnut and, after it was gone, drank coffee. "No, I don't think so."

"Do you have any idea why someone would want to kill him?"

"In all honesty, Reece, I do not."

"Any speculation?"

"We could play what if all day long and not hit the truth."

"True that. Do you own any knives?"

Harry raised an eyebrow. "Are you scraping the bottom of the barrel?"

"Gotta ask all manner of questions."

"Aside from kitchen knives, I do own a few. I'm not big into knives, that's why it's only a few."

"Any of your knives made of stone?"

Harry's eyes opened wide. "Did you say *stone*?"

"Yes."

"No. No, stone knives."

Reece stared at his notebook. *This isn't getting me anywhere. His guard is up.*

Turning his attention back to Harry, he asked, "May I have a cup of coffee?"

"Oh, goodness. Where are my manners? Sure. Kenya Double A good?"

"Sure."

He watched Harry signal to Estrelita.

"Mind if I ask *you* a question?"

Reece shook his head. "No. Ask."

"Has it been established if Humphrey's murder was done by the Full Moon Killer?"

"It has, and the answer is no. But that's not for publication."

"Okay. Now I understand why you're asking these questions. For the record, neither Em nor I murdered the man."

"Noted."

Estrelita set the cup of coffee before Reece, and he allowed her to pour some cream into the cup. She asked if there was anything else, and when he said no, she left.

He drank the golden liquid, closed his eyes for a moment, and savored the rich flavor.

When he opened them, he saw Harry looking at him with a smirk on his face.

"What?"

"Is it good?"

"More than good, it's—"

Harry held up a hand. "Don't say it."

Reece threw his head back, and a laugh rumbled from his gut. Laugh gone, but still chuckling, he said, "Okay. I won't."

Harry held up his cup. "Simple pleasures are best. They bring the most happiness."

"Yes, they do."

The two men touched cups.

Harry went on to say, "People see me as vain and a showoff because of my clothes and cars. And perhaps I am. They do, though, bring me a lot of pleasure. In a way, they're like art."

"Huh. Never thought of clothes as art. Cars maybe."

"But the best pleasure is sitting in my rocking chair on the porch in the autumn with a hot cup of coffee and my old Jobey pipe that I bought for ten bucks twenty years ago."

Reece drank coffee. "I getcha. Don't get to do it much, but for me, it's walking in the woods with my dog."

"One of these days, we should go for a walk together."

"Really?"

"Sure. Why not?"

Reece smiled. "Yeah. Why not?"

He sat there drinking coffee with Harry until the cup was empty.

"Well, I'd best be going. Murders don't solve themselves."

"Very true, Sarge."

Reece smiled at that, rose, and left. Out on the sidewalk, he took a cigar out of his pocket, removed the cellophane, and sank his teeth into it.

*I must be getting soft in my old age. Walking with Thurgood.*

He shook his head and briskly took off down the sidewalk, headed towards the police station.

# 51

## TUESDAY, JANUARY 14, 3:44 PM

MBPD OFFICER HELEN BEAUREGARD sat in a chair on the other side of the desk from the Reverend Ember Cole.

She didn't know the controversial minister, but seeing her up close, the woman made for a different impression than the one gained from listening to the gossips.

Ember Cole wasn't tall. On the shorter side of average. She wore a simple black A-line dress with clerical collar. The gold pectoral cross and wedding ring, her only jewelry. She appeared to be wearing no makeup.

*Rather than her physical presence,* Helen thought, *it's her quiet demeanor that makes the most impact. It's as though you feel the calmness and peace of a satisfied soul radiating off her.*

Helen cleared her throat and began. "Sergeant Sovern asked me to ask you a few questions about the murder of your assistant pastor."

"Okay. Let's get the big one out of the way first. I didn't kill him."

Helen smiled. "All right. I got that one down. Do you have any idea as to who might want him dead?"

"No, I don't. I find it difficult to imagine someone resorting to murder to solve a problem."

"Yet, they do."

"Especially since that writer group held their retreat here."

Helen wasn't sure what Reverend Cole was talking about, but she made a note of it, and would visit it later if she had to.

"Ms. Cole, there's no one in your church who didn't like the man? I find that difficult to believe."

"I don't believe I said that. Yes, there are some who didn't like him. I, for one, didn't like him."

"You didn't like him, yet he was your assistant pastor."

"We needed someone to fill the pulpit. The bishop sent him to us, and the church council asked the bishop to assign him as our assistant pastor, which he did."

"Without asking you?"

"It's basically up to the bishop. But even though there are those here who didn't like Reverend Humphrey, there are many who loved him. He wasn't impossible to work with, so I decided to just live with the situation. And in the end, he would've proven to be very useful, so I'm sorry he's gone. He will be deeply missed by a lot of people."

"But not you."

"I didn't say that. He would've been useful in the ministry here, so I will miss him. Besides, what happened to him was horrible. And I hope his killer is found and justice is handed out. Reverend Humphrey deserves justice."

"I'm with you there. We need a lead, though. Right now, we're kind of lost in the woods."

"Was he a victim of the Full Moon Killer?"

"I'm not at liberty to say, Reverend."

"Of course not. Did you see today's *Chronicle*?"

"No, I haven't read it yet."

"Well, Graham has in one day on two and a half pages given us more than the police have, in what, seven months? With Adelbert's death, this is coming home and people want to know what's going on."

"I understand. But I don't set policy."

"I know you don't. However, I can't help but wonder if the police and sheriff opened up, they might get some valuable information from the people."

"I'm not going to argue with you, Reverend. But I'm here talking to you about the murder of Reverend Humphrey. What can *you* tell me that might help us solve the case?"

Helen watched Ember lean back in her chair and close her eyes.

*Is she praying? Concocting a story? Talking to Jesus? That was part of the gossip. The prostitute and pornstar that talks to Jesus. Although I find it difficult to imagine the woman sitting before me was a pornstar.*

Reverend Cole opened her eyes and sat up. "Adelbert never said he was gay, but most everyone thought he was. And I think the manner in which he was mutilated indicates that his killer is someone who is anti-gay, or was an angry lover or former lover. That's the line of inquiry I'd pursue if I were you. Or Reece. That's the best advice I can give."

*She called him Reece. So the rumors are true that she and her husband are friends with the Soverns.*

"Okay, Reverend, I'll pass that on to Sergeant Sovern."

Helen closed her notebook, cleared her throat, and said, "I'd like to ask a personal question. If you don't want to answer it, no problem."

A smile appeared on Ember's lips. "Ask and you may receive."

"Were you really a pornstar? I mean, you don't look like one, physically, I mean."

Helen was surprised when she heard the minister burst into a hearty laugh.

She said, "Yes, I was a pornstar. My boyish figure enabled me to play the little girl, and a lot of men like that. Women, too."

"Seriously?"

"Seriously."

"Oh, wow. That's just... And women?"

"Uh-huh. A mom teaching her daughter? Oh, yeah. But that person is dead. She died when she gave her heart to Jesus. I'm a new creation in Christ."

"You really believe that?"

"Yes, I do. Overnight, I gave up the sex, the booze, the drugs, the cigarettes, the money. I became a disciple of my Lord and Savior. I truly became a new person. Overnight. And you can, too, Helen."

"How do you know I'm not a churchgoer?"

"I know. You were baptized Catholic. Stopped going to church when you went to college. Were Baptist for a short time to make the guy you were dating happy. And when you broke up with him, you quit going to church again."

Helen was astonished. How did she know this? "Uh, well, I was unaware that you possessed such detailed knowledge about me. Who told you? My mother?"

"No. I haven't met your mother. Jesus told me. He's calling you through me to come home."

"Oh, wow. This is too much." Helen stood. "Okay, I'm leaving now."

Helen headed for the door. Behind her, she heard Ember speaking.

"Remember, Helen, 'His yoke is easy, and His burden is light.' Don't forget."

Once out of the office, Officer Helen Beauregard ran out of the church, and entering her car, slammed the door shut and made sure it was locked.

"Holy shit, that was weird. She's as kooky as that woman who sells those crystals. Reece and GJ can tackle her next time, because I'm never going back."

# 52

## TUESDAY, JANUARY 14, 4:02 PM

TIPPER DUVALL DID NOT ENJOY HAVING tea with Mary Lou Fight. And she liked it even less when little Mary Lou, which was what everyone called Oralene, was present.

Today was her unlucky day. Both big and little Mary Lou were present.

Mary Lou set her teacup on the saucer and set both on the coffee table.

"This is not at all satisfactory, Tipper. The bishop is not taking my calls. You will need to tell him we need an assistant pastor who will meet our needs as Reverend Humphrey did."

"Yes, ma'am."

"And tell him we aren't in a rush. We want the right candidate. We *deserve* to have the best he has available."

"Yes, ma'am. I will."

"Why anyone would want to murder that kind and gentle man is impossible to understand."

"It's a shock to all of us," Tipper said.

"He was a Sodomite," Oralene said, as though she was announcing it was raining when everyone should have already known.

Mary Lou turned to her adopted daughter. "What did you say?"

"He was a Sodomite, Mother. God destroyed Sodom and Gomorrah. His holy wrath burns against those who lust after their own kind. God destroyed him. I don't think we should weep. As it says in the Good Book: 'Thou shalt break them with a rod of iron. Thou shalt dash them in pieces, like a potter's vessel.' You should not weep. You should rejoice. God has removed sin from his holy temple."

Tipper's eyebrows shot up as she listened to the ignorant fundamentalism of Little Mary Lou, and at the same time watched Mary Lou's eyes narrow.

*I bet she regrets adopting her. That one is a dangerous handful.*

"Then why hasn't He removed the strumpet?" Mary Lou said, biting off each word.

"God's ways are not our ways. Be patient, Mother. The rod will dash her in pieces as well." Oralene picked up her teacup and drank.

Tipper was dumbfounded by what she was hearing. *That girl is nuts. Certifiably crazy. What the hell was Mary Lou thinking of when she adopted* her*?*

---

Ember looked at the hands on her Art Deco Bulova desk clock, a gift from Harry. She didn't need a desk clock. She had the date and time on her computer, as well as on her phone. But she'd accepted it with grace. There was, though, a simple elegance about it that she did find appealing.

The hands told her there wasn't much more she could do at her desk than she could do at home, so she opted for home.

She put her laptop, a couple legal pads, and a book into the dark brown leather attaché (which was another gift from Harry), slipped into her coat, and put the strap over her shoulder along with her black slim purse.

At the door, she turned off the office light, told Larrilyn good night and walked out the front of the church.

After a moment's thought, she decided to walk down to the Really Good and catch a ride with Harry.

Making sure the church doors were securely closed, Fred would lock them later, she turned and headed for the sidewalk.

Out of the corner of her eye she noticed movement, looked up, saw the old rusty pickup truck slow down, and an arm extend from the window.

When Ember realized what was in the hand at the end of that arm, she exclaimed, "Oh, Jesus," just as the bullets started flying.

# 53

## TUESDAY, JANUARY 14, 6:31 PM

I COULD NOT RELAX. I sat. Then got up and paced. Returned to my chair, only to get up again forty-five seconds later.

With me was Graham Huston. He was at the shop to pick up his supper when the phone call came. And Reece Sovern joined us shortly after Graham and I arrived at the hospital.

"You're making me nervous, Harry," Graham said. "Sit."

"Somebody shot Em."

"Look, I spent years having my buddies and myself shot at, and some of them died. I didn't. Die, that is. Although there are days I wish I had. I can tell you, pacing isn't going to help."

Reece said, "Save it, Huston. He ain't listening."

"I suppose you're right," I said, "but this is Em. The mother of our kids. I understand there are people out there who don't like her, but enough to kill her?"

Reece slid his glasses back up to the top of his nose. "You've told me many times people will kill each other for five bucks."

I collapsed into a chair. "So I have. And now it's come home to roost."

"You know," Graham began, "I really don't like hospitals. They're cold and impersonal."

Reece snorted a laugh. "What do you want? A fireplace and a tumbler of Blue Corn at your elbow?"

"That's a start," Graham answered.

Reece reached out and put a hand on my shoulder. "She's going to be okay."

My elbows were on my knees and my hands on either side of my head. "You don't know that."

His butt moved to the edge of the chair and he turned so he could face me. His hands were on his knees. "I talked with the ambulance crew."

I sat up and looked him in the eyes. "And you're just telling me this now? What did they say?"

"She appeared to have only minor injuries."

"Appeared?"

He sat back in the chair. "She was dazed and shaken, and the crew didn't spend time on a full exam. They saw no major bleeding. So we can be thankful for that. Although that leather bag is trash."

"Her attaché?"

"I guess. Nice leather job. Well, it was nice."

"Huh. Like those stories of a guy saved by the Bible in his pocket," Graham added.

Reece nodded. "Yeah. Like that."

"Thanks for telling me," I said. "I hope they're right."

Reece once again put his hand on my shoulder. "It's their job to make those assessments."

I nodded.

"The medics were lifesavers," Graham said. "They weren't doctors, but they could've been."

There was a lull in our talking. The sounds of the hospital were more apparent. Or perhaps I should say, the lack thereof.

Burnet Medical Center is located on the other side of the college. It's a small acute care facility, but has quite a bit of modern equipment. Even boasts a helipad. I hoped Reece was right and we wouldn't need it.

A voice broke the silence. "There you are."

I looked up, stood, and shook hands with Dr. Ram Patel, the medical director.

"Isn't it your quitting time?" I said.

He laughed. "Doctors have no quitting time." Then he turned serious. "I heard Reverend Cole had been shot. I stuck around in case Dr. Thorne needed help."

"Do you know how she is?"

"She's in excellent hands. Winthrop Thorne saw far worse than this in Afghanistan. He'll be out soon to give you an update."

"But she is okay," I pressed.

"I believe so, but I'll let Thorne give you the lowdown."

"Thanks, Doc."

"Don't mention it. Now I am going home."

We shook hands and Patel left.

Graham stood and stretched. "As I said, she'll be okay."

On the heels of Graham's comment, a somewhat portly, fifty-something man wearing a white coat walked into the waiting area.

"Harry Thurgood?" he said.

"I'm Thurgood."

"Mr. Thurgood, I'm Winthrop Thorne. I treated your wife."

That elevated him in my book. I have added respect for a doctor who doesn't call himself doctor.

"How is she?" I asked.

"Somewhat shaken. I gave her a mild sedative to keep her calm and to help her sleep. Physically, she has scraps on her hands and a bruised knee due to sidewalk impact. A bullet also grazed her rib cage. Might leave a scar. Hopefully not. She's all bandaged up and you can take her home. I don't see any need to keep her overnight. Although we can do so if you wish. But I think she'll be better at home."

"Thanks, doctor."

Reece and Graham were both taking notes. Albeit for different purposes. At least, that was my guess.

"She was a lucky woman. If that bullet had slipped between the ribs, it would be a different story."

"What size bullet?" I asked.

"The police can tell you more. I'm guessing a thirty-eight. Perhaps fired from a snub-nosed revolver. Longer barrel and the bullet would've had more punch. Again, a lucky woman."

"Thanks, doc. What room?"

"Number one. Have a good night."

Thorne left, and the three of us walked down the gleaming white corridor to Em's room.

When Reece saw her eyes were closed, he whispered, "I'll talk to her tomorrow."

To Graham, he nodded his head towards the door.

Graham gave my shoulder a squeeze and left with Reece.

I sat on the bed, and she opened her eyes.

Her voice was groggy. "Hi, handsome."

"Hey, beautiful."

"Jesus saved me. He got between me and the truck and pushed me to the sidewalk."

I took her hand and gave it a squeeze. "I'm glad."

"Can I go home?"

"You can. You want to?"

"Yes. Max and Monette."

"Okay. Let's get you home."

She closed her eyes, and I pressed the button for the nurse.

*Whoever did this is going to rue the day they were born.*

# 54

## TUESDAY, JANUARY 14, 8:04 PM

Reece Sovern was sitting behind his desk looking at the forensics report. GJ occupied a chair on the other side, reading over the printed copies of the statements she'd collected.

Four bullets, thirty-eight special jacketed hollow points, hit the attaché bag and were stopped by the laptop and a book. The fifth got through and wounded the Reverend.

Because the hollow points hadn't expanded, the weapon was probably a small, five-round J-Frame revolver. A Saturday Night Special.

Reece put the report down. *She was indeed lucky,* he told himself, then muttered, "Moron didn't know his weapon. Thank God."

"What was that, Sarge?"

"Oh, just saying the shooter was a moron to load jacketed hollow points in a little J-Frame and not shoot her at close range. Saved the Reverend's life, though."

"Lucky for her."

"And the babies. And her husband."

"And all the people in her congregation, and the good folk of Magnolia Bluff."

"You don't like her."

"Can't say I do."

"Why?"

"Miss Goody Two-Shoes. And her husband? He'd steal my five-year-old nephew's bag of Legos if he had half a chance. He's a shady, smarmy character if there ever was one. The word around town is that Mrs. Fight calls him a lounge lizard. Probably was — and maybe still is — a gigolo. I bet that's how he got his money. Diddling old women. Maybe old men, too."

Reece took his glasses off and pinched the bridge of his nose.

"Have a headache, Sarge? Let me massage your temples for you."

He put his glasses back on. "I'm all right. What did you discover? Anyone witness the shooting?"

"No one saw anything. A couple thought a car was backfiring. Old people. Do cars even backfire these days?"

Reece thought for a moment. "Can't say they do. Mine haven't."

"One person said the time was..." She looked through the statements. "Here it is. 'About a quarter past four.' Who even talks that way anymore?"

"That person does. So at least we have a time. Nothing on the truck?"

"One man was sitting on his porch, smoking his pipe, and said he must've dozed off. The backfires, he thought they were backfires, woke him and he saw an old, rusted Chevy pickup driving pretty fast down the street away from the Methodist Church."

"Did he get a license plate number? Color? Year?"

"No plate number. No color. Just rusted and sun bleached. And old. No year. Admitted he doesn't know much about pickups."

Reece shook his head. "People used to notice things. Not anymore. Okay. An old, rusted, sun-bleached pickup. How many of them do you suppose are in the county?"

GJ screwed her face up in thought. "Probably a lot more fifty years ago from the way my dad and Uncle Waymon talk. Today, not so much. More and more people with money moving here."

Reece nodded. "True. It takes a few million to start up one of those fancy wineries. Put out an APB for the pickup. Hopefully, someone knows something about it. And pass the info on to Buck's people. For now, that's all the time we can spend on this case. The Full Moon Murderer is still out there."

"I talked with the realtors in town." She looked through her notebook. "I got names of eleven buyers and four renters."

Reece looked at his watch. "Okay. Good. We'll start on them in the morning."

"This is as bad as trying to get out of old Otto Velmer's corn maze when I was a kid."

Reece snorted a laugh. "He made some good ones. I remember—"

His desk phone rang and interrupted the story he was about to tell. He picked up the handset.

"Sovern."

"Hi, Reece. This is Joyce Blackstone."

"Evening, Joyce."

"I took a quick look through the *Chronicle* just now and saw something about some group called the New Order of the Crimson Dawn."

"Okay."

"The name rang a bell, so I checked my listings. I didn't sell the property, but I listed it and—"

"GJ and I will be at your place in ten."

"Uh, probably not a good idea."

"Oh. Brandon's there. All right, why don't you come down to the station?"

"I can be there in twenty minutes."

"Good. GJ and I will be waiting."

# 55

## TUESDAY, JANUARY 14, 9:09 PM

A CLERK SHOWED Joyce Blackstone to Reece Sovern's office.

Reece and GJ stood when she entered. "Evening, Joyce," he said. "Have a seat."

She smiled to herself as she sat. *What a contrast those two make.*

Reece had on blue-gray slacks, a light blue shirt with no necktie, and a dark blue graph check sport coat. She guessed the coat and slacks had last been pressed sometime during the Vietnam War.

GJ sported a midnight blue pants suit, white blouse, and a narrow gray tie. Joyce guessed they were fresh from the cleaners. The creases were very sharp.

Reece sat behind his desk and GJ was off to the side, so both were facing her. He pushed his glasses back up to the top of his nose and said, "Thanks for coming. What do you have for us?"

"Fifteen months ago, I listed the Adolf Bauer farm for sale."

"Wasn't that place abandoned property?"

"Yes, and no. Old Mister Bauer left no will. He had no immediate family. At least not in the area. The court then tried to track down the closest living relative. They finally found him around two years ago. A fourth cousin, x number of times removed. The cousin came to look over the property, and didn't even get all the way down the drive when he turned around, showed up at our office, and said, 'Sell it.'

"I got the listing. But it was a realtor in San Antonio who represented the buyer. A lawyer for the New Order of the Crimson Dawn."

GJ, her face flint, her voice broken glass, asked, "You have names and addresses?"

Joyce felt the hostility rolling off the woman, but chose to ignore it. She smiled and said, her voice bright, "I do." She then reached into her handbag, took out a sheet of paper, and put it on Reece's desk. "Names, addresses, and phone numbers are all there."

Reece picked up the sheet. He spent a moment looking at it, then put it down and smiled at her. "Thanks, Joyce. Hopefully, this proves to be the break we need."

"Good. Glad I could be of at least potential help."

GJ cut in. "Be sure to keep that boyfriend of yours on a leash. Captain Briggs doesn't welcome private snoops."

Joyce stood. "Brandon isn't a private snoop. He's a retired police officer."

GJ stood and continued, "And one who keeps horning in on police business — which is what private snoops like to do. Tell him to stick to divorce cases."

"Look here, Officer—"

Reece jumped up. "Look, ladies, we don't want a verbal brawl here. GJ, Joyce was kind enough to come to us with potentially valuable information. If this helps us solve the case, Briggs will be happy as a deer in a cornfield."

Joyce watched GJ change her stance, so it was no longer aggressive. She looked Joyce in the face, but not the eyes.

"Excuse me, ma'am. I was just trying to make clear Captain Briggs's policy."

"Oh, it's clear, Officer," Joyce said. She faced Reece. "You might want to let your captain know I'll be taking this up with the Civilian Advisory Board."

"Now, Joyce—"

"No, Reece. The new guy on the block has crossed the line. If I happen to come across any other information, I'll pass it on to *you* and only *you*. Goodnight."

---

Reece watched Joyce leave. When she was gone, he sat.

"The bacon's in the fire now," he said.

GJ sat. "I'm sorry, Sarge. Guess I got my tit in the wringer on that one."

Reece raised his eyebrows, coughed, and said, "Uh, you could put it that way."

"I let my emotions get carried away."

"Yes, you did. And now we're going to hear about it. Because even though the policy is Briggs's, the road apples never fall up. Only down. It will be our fault. 'We misunderstood his directive. We were over zealous in following his orders.' Or some such bull crap."

"I'll take the blame, Sarge. I don't want—"

Reece put his hand up. "Nonsense. I'm your boss and I'll handle it. Just promise me you'll bite your tongue and count to ten the next time. Promise me?"

"I promise, Sarge."

"Good. We don't like the guy, you and I, but the chief apparently does. We have to keep that in mind. After all, the chief is the chief. And Briggs is only a captain."

"Gotcha."

"I think we're done here. Let's go home."

"Uh, Sarge, can I buy you a drink to make up for my screw up?"

Reece paused a moment before saying, "Thanks, GJ, but I'm going to pass. I'm tired and would like to hit the hay."

"Another time, perhaps?"

"Sure. And don't be so hard on yourself. Mistakes are part of the job. And pubic relations is the crappiest part of the job."

"Okay. Thanks, Sarge. Goodnight."

Reece watched her go. He picked up his hat and coat, then set them down. He closed his door and got resettled in his chair. In the bottom drawer, on the right side of the desk, was a special bottle.

He opened the drawer, took out the bottle of Garrison Cowboy and a tumbler, poured himself two fingers of two hundred dollar bourbon, and took a sip.

Holding the glass up to the light, letting it filter through the amber fluid, he said, "This ain't a special occasion, but I just might need you to help me weather the coming storm."

---

Scarlett Hayden tossed back a third of her martini, then hurled the glass against the wall.

*That damn woman is still alive. What is she? A cat? Why can't she die? Harry is mine. Mine! I deserve him. Not her. Yet she has him. And now they have a couple of brats. He'll never leave her. Why can't she die? Shit. What do I need to use? A bazooka?*

Scarlett walked to her bar and made herself another martini. She took a large swallow and carried the glass to the sofa.

From out of a drawer in the end table, she retrieved a picture she'd taken of Harry.

"I can say this. You got lucky, Ember Cole. Damn lucky. But one of these days, your luck is going to run out. And when it does, and you're at the bottom of the Reservoir, your man will be mine. Mine! And your little brats, too."

Scarlett took a large swallow of her drink and kissed the picture of Harry Thurgood.

Whispering, she said, "I love you, Harry Thurgood. And I will do anything to get you. Anything. The days of your pretty little call girl are numbered. Enjoy her while you can. But you'll be surprised at what a real woman can give you. And I can't wait to give it to you."

## 56

### TUESDAY, JANUARY 14, 11:18 PM

I CAN'T SLEEP. And rather than disturb Em with my tossing and turning, I got up and sat by the fire; a Corpse Reviver No. 1, my pipe, and Princess my companions.

Although with the sedative, probably nothing short of a nuclear blast would wake my bride.

I took a sip of my drink and puffed on my pipe. The flames danced around the new logs I'd put on the dying embers.

*Who would want to shoot Em?* That was the question I kept asking myself and I kept coming up with the same answer: unknown.

A shooting was not Mary Lou Fight's style. But maybe it was Oralene's. I hadn't forgotten the threat she'd made against us.

I picked up my phone and sent a text to Reece to check on alibis for Oralene and her brothers. Moments later, a thumbs up emoticon came through.

"Huh. You're still up," I said out loud. Princess lifted her head. I told her I wasn't talking to her and her head settled back down between her paws.

Reece is a hard worker, and I think the FBI training he received has honed his investigative skills for major crimes.

Where are we, though, in all of this? Have we gotten any closer to solving these cases?

I chuckled at my use of the word "we."

"You aren't involved, Harry, remember?" Then I thought of Em. And the anger surged through me, strong and terrible, a Force 10 gale. "Yes, you are involved. At least where Em is concerned."

I took a large swallow of my drink, paused, took a deep breath and exhaled, then puffed on my pipe and gazed at the fire.

My mind drifted back to my initial question: who wanted Em dead? Dead enough that he or she would do a drive-by shooting?

The flames gave back no answer, nor did the smoke from my pipe. Nevertheless, my mind kept circling back to Oralene and her threat to us.

There was something definitely wrong with that girl. And being Mary Lou's protégé wasn't going to improve her one little bit.

But what could I actually do to bring justice for Em?

I puffed on my pipe, took a swallow of my drink, and puffed some more.

There was only one avenue open to me. I needed to talk to Reece. I needed to know what he knew. I needed all the puzzle pieces collected to date on all the murders to see if I saw something our esteemed gendarmes had missed. To see if the Full Moon Killer was involved with Em's shooting, or if the shooting was related to Humphrey's murder, or if hers was a totally separate case. And if totally separate, to discover who so hated her, they felt compelled to eliminate her.

And a talk with Elisha Reston to see if he'd spill the beans on his sister probably wasn't a bad idea either.

# 57

## WEDNESDAY, JANUARY 15, 5:49 AM

Reece agreed to meet me at the coffee shop to discuss the murders and attempted murder. He arrived at quarter to six, as agreed. I had a cup of coffee waiting for him.

"Thanks, Harry. Appreciate the cup of joe."

"It's the least I can do for getting you up so early."

"Unfortunately, not so early for me. A murder, attempted murder, and a serial killer. No rest for the wicked or the just." He took a sip of coffee, sighing in contentment, and asked, "So what's on your mind?"

"I need to be a part of these investigations."

"Doubt Briggs will be amenable to that."

"I could appeal to the chief."

"You could. But he hired Briggs."

"I could appeal to the mayor."

Reece nodded and sipped coffee. "Heard tell you made a big donation to his campaign fund. Might get you somewhere."

"But I'd rather not call in that favor."

I watched his face turn thoughtful while he drank coffee. After a few moments, he said, "Could I trouble you for a piece of pie to go with this coffee?"

"Sure." I got up, got him a slice of apple pie with a hunk of cheddar cheese, and topped up his coffee.

"Well, if that don't beat all. Thanks for the cheese. Don't see that very often these days."

"Thought you might like that. How about you just share with me where you're currently at? Just friends talking."

Reece snorted a laugh. "Yeah, Briggs doesn't want us discussing anything with civilians." He took a bite of pie and followed it with a bite of cheese. "My God, Harry, where did you get this cheese? Not even Kroger sells anything like this."

"Special order from upstate New York. Aged for ten years."

Reece shook his head. "Okay. With cheese like this, if I can have more, what do you want to know?"

I laughed. "That was easy. And yes, you can have more."

Reece slid his glasses back up to the top of his nose and got a forkful of pie into his mouth. When it was gone, he followed it with a bite of cheese. When that was on its way south, he said, "To be honest, I'm still pissed at Briggs for arresting Annie Kate. So what do you want to know?"

"Where to start?" I composed my thoughts, then began. "Em. Is the attempt on her life related to the murder of Humphrey or the Full Moon Murders?"

"No, on the Full Moon Murders. I think that is a definite. Neither the Humphrey murder, nor the attempt on your wife, are connected to the serial killings. The question that's not fully resolved is, are Ember and Humphrey related?"

"In your opinion, are they?"

Reece drank coffee, ate pie and cheese, and shrugged. "Both are connected to the church. Although Humphrey looks like a hate crime and Ember more like an assassination attempt. The means are different in the two cases. Humphrey was a crude attempt to mimic the Full Moon Killer. Whereas it looks like a straight up drive by for Ember."

I drank coffee and filed the information away.

"So, what can *you* tell *me*? You must've heard something from that gossip group that meets here every morning."

I gave him a wry smile. "Not a whole lot. Wild rumors mostly."

"How wild?"

"Everything from space aliens to the Mafia to gangs coming down from Dallas and Fort Worth."

Reece snorted a laugh. "Sounds about right."

"Graham hasn't received a response from his notice in the paper yesterday."

"You expect him to?" Reece drank coffee and finished his pie and cheese.

I paused, then said, "Do you?"

"No. Quite honestly, I doubt if there are any of those nutters here. I think they pick a town, conduct a few ritualistic murders, and then move on."

"If that's the case, you're going to have to try to track the comings and goings of a whole lot of people in order to find the culprits."

"True that. We'll see if the real estate purchases produce a lead. If they don't, we're going to be going after airlines, car rental companies, ride sharing outfits, and the bus companies in an effort to track down visitors who might be part of this group."

"Any luck from the Rangers?"

"They've been working the web angle, but so far they've been stymied by the shell companies. Whoever created this group was pretty tech and legal savvy. It's no Tom, Dick, and Harry outfit." He paused a moment and then said, "Just saying."

I smiled. "I know."

"For what it's worth, I think we're dealing with three different perps: the Full Moon Killer; someone who doesn't like homosexuals in the pulpit, hence the mutilation and dumping of the body on your land to send a message; and someone who has it in for your wife to the point where now they want to kill her."

"You have an alibi for Mary Lou and Oralene?"

"I'll be talking to them today. Probably won't get anywhere, but I'll talk to them. And on that note—"

He stood. "I'd best get going. Got some killers to catch."

I stood as well, extended my hand, and we shook hands.

Reece gave me a smile. "We'll talk again."

"Thanks, Sarge."

He stuck the Zeppelin pipe in his mouth, angled it upward, gave me a lazy salute, and left.

*I like Reece. We got off to a rocky start, but he's a good cop. Still not overly imaginative. But he's getting there. And with a little help from his friends, he's got this.*

# 58

## WEDNESDAY, JANUARY 15, 9:06 AM

REECE AND GJ were sitting in a cubical on the other side of the desk from Maria Santos, a realtor with the Jenny Diamond Realty Group. The same realtor who had found the Adolf Bauer farm for Dorcas Wheeler, Esquire, operating as the agent for the New Order of the Crimson Dawn.

Maria Santos began. "You say you are police officers from Magnolia Bluff investigating a case?"

"Yes, ma'am," Reece said.

"Do you mind if I see your ID?"

"No, ma'am," Reece answered.

He and GJ showed the agent their police IDs. After a moment, she nodded and asked how she could help them.

GJ said, "Ten months ago you purchased a property, the Adolf Bauer farm, for the New Order of the Crimson Dawn through their agent, Dorcas Wheeler, Esquire, a lawyer with the firm of Kashdan, Goldman, Pocket, and Cash in New York City."

Maria Santos nodded. "Yes. Ms. Wheeler saw the property, took pictures with her phone, sent them to her client, and after some texting, said her client would buy the property for the asking price."

"Sweet deal," Reece said.

"Yes. That doesn't happen very often for a place in the condition that farm was in."

"Anything unusual about the sale?" Reece asked.

"The lawyer handled everything, which in and of itself isn't odd, but what was different, something I'd never seen before, was her paying the three hundred and fifty thousand dollars in cash. All one hundred dollar bills."

"Wow," GJ said, "that must've been a sight."

"Two suitcases. I had no idea cash could be so heavy."

"Where did the money come from?" Reece asked.

The real estate agent shrugged. "The lawyer didn't say. We all showed up at Joyce Blackstone's office and Ms. Wheeler lugged in the suitcases and told us there would be no need for a mortgage and that her client wished to take possession immediately."

"And you never learned anything about the buyer?" GJ asked.

"The lawyer was the buyer's agent, so we didn't need to know anything about the buyer. But I didn't even learn much about the lawyer. She wasn't given to small talk and was all business. And I mean *all* business."

Reece stood. "Thank you for your help, Ms. Santos. Here's my card. Please call if you think of anything about the sale that you didn't mention today. No matter what it is."

GJ and Ms. Santos stood, and the realtor assured Reece she would get in touch if she thought of anything.

On the drive back to Magnolia Bluff, GJ observed, "You know, Sarge, I don't have a good feeling about this case."

"How so?"

"These Crimson Dawn people are too good. There's no place we can get a wedge in to pry this thing apart."

"True. That's how it seems. But unless these people aren't people, they're eventually going to make a mistake and we'd better be there when they do."

# 59

## WEDNESDAY, JANUARY 15, 9:16 AM

EMBER PARKED in front of the Magnolia Bluff Real Estate Agency, where Joyce Blackstone worked.

She'd called the *Chronicle* earlier and Monika told her no Crimson Dawn members had called or shown up at the office.

"Two publicity seekers showed up," Monika said, "but Graham shooed them out."

So, on a whim, Ember decided she'd check with Joyce to find out if her favorite realtor might have any information.

Her side ached where the bullet had plowed what was sure to be a scar across her rib cage. Clara had been opposed to her going out. Clucking like a mother hen about rest and taking it easy. But Ember had no desire to take it easy. There was too much to do and not enough life to do it in, as the aching wound reminded her.

She got out of her car and entered the agency, asking the receptionist if Joyce was in.

A moment later, she was led back to her friend's cubicle.

"So what can I do for you, Reverend?" Joyce asked once they were seated.

"We've known each other long enough. Ember, or Em, is perfectly all right."

Joyce smiled. "I'll try to remember, but seeing that collar just makes me think of Reverend."

Ember chuckled. "It does have that effect on people."

"So how can I help you?"

Ember leaned forward. "I'm here on a snooping mission and I wonder if you can help?"

Joyce leaned forward. "I can try. What are you snooping? Wait, let me guess. The Full Moon Murders."

"Yes. Can you tell me who bought property here a year ago?"

"I can do better than that. I can give you what I gave Reece Sovern."

"You can?"

Joyce nodded.

"That's fabulous."

"But should you be up and about having just been shot?"

"Flesh wound. I'll probably get an ugly scar out of it and nothing more."

Joyce laughed. "Oh, just an ugly scar. Listen to you."

She opened a desk drawer and took out a sheet of paper. Grabbing a notepad, she copied the information that was on the paper, tore off the sheet from the pad, and handed it to her friend.

"Thanks, Joyce."

"Now don't get yourself in trouble over this."

"I won't. Can you give me directions to this place?"

Joyce looked at her watch. "Better yet, I can show you. I have an hour and a half before my appointment. We can go in my car."

"Sounds good. Let's go."

---

The women exited the car.

Ember said, "This place is out in the middle of nowhere."

"Old abandoned farms are either on the edge of town, being

overrun by urbanization, or they are like this — out in the middle of nowhere."

The breeze blew dust whorls across what was once the front yard.

Ember shivered. "Kind of spooky."

"It is at that. Well, now that we're here, what are you going to do?"

"Snoop."

"Seriously?"

"Yep. If this place is owned by that cult group and they're behind this current spate of murders, then we might find some evidence here."

"You sound just like Brandon. Can't leave things alone."

"You can thank our good friend, Reece, for bringing out my inner detective."

"I guess he arrested you one time too many."

"You got that right, sister."

The two women laughed.

"I'm going up to the front door and knock. See if anyone's home. You coming?"

Joyce hesitated a moment, then nodded and followed Ember.

They climbed the three steps to the porch, crossed to the front door, and Ember knocked.

In response to her rapping on the wood, the door inched inward.

The women looked at each other, then Ember pushed the door open and called out, "Hello. Anybody home?"

When no answer came to her question, Ember crossed the threshold.

"Hello," she called again. "Anybody here?"

She waited for a reply, and when none came, she slowly stepped into the entryway, which was actually a short hallway.

On her right was a closed door and stairs going up to the second floor. On her left was a glass wall and a door. The room looked to be the living room. Straight ahead was another closed door.

She turned and motioned for Joyce to enter.

"I don't like this," Joyce said in a stage whisper as she stepped into the hallway.

No lights were on in the hall or the living room. Light filtered in through the open front door. Shades had been pulled over the living room windows. No light came from the room.

"Just a minute, Joyce. Let me turn on my phone's flashlight."

Ember fished her phone out of her purse and the light came on.

At the same time, the door ahead of them opened and the door by the stairs opened.

Two women, wearing ankle-length cream-colored dresses, fitted at the waist, with puff shoulders, and high collars, stepped through the doorways.

The one in front of Ember spoke. "Well, well, Mrs. Galt, it looks as though the mountain has come to Mohammed."

"Or, Mrs. Faber, perhaps it's a case of the flies coming to the spider."

# 60

## WEDNESDAY, JANUARY 15, 11:31 AM

BRANDON TURNER WALKED into Magnolia Bluff Real Estate. To the receptionist, he said, "Joyce show up?"

"No. One of the other agents was free and filled in for her. This isn't like her not to show up for an appointment."

"Did she come in at all?"

"Yes. She was here and left a couple of hours ago with Reverend Cole."

"Any idea where they went?"

The receptionist shook her head. "Joyce didn't say. Just that she'd be back."

"That's not like her."

"No, it isn't. That's why I called you."

"Thanks. And you called her?"

"Yes. But she's not answering her phone. I've left a couple messages, but she hasn't called back."

"And *that's* not like her."

Brandon tried his girlfriend's number, and the call went to voicemail. He said, "Hey, Sweetie, hope everything's okay. Call me when you get this."

He put his phone in his pocket, took it out again and told it to call Harry Thurgood.

The coffee shop owner answered on the third ring. "Hi, Brandon. What can I do you for?"

"Have you heard from Ember?"

"No. Why?"

"She and Joyce took off to somewhere, and then Joyce missed her eleven o'clock appointment. Plus, she isn't answering her phone."

"Huh. Hang on. Let me call Em."

Brandon heard the phone go silent. In a minute, Harry was back.

"You there?"

"I'm here. Anything?"

"No. She didn't answer her cell or her desk phone. That's not like her."

"Something's up. Harry."

"You've no idea where they went?"

"Correct. The receptionist said Joyce didn't tell her where she was going."

"Anything on her desk to indicate where they might have gone?"

"Let me check."

Brandon quickly walked to Joyce's desk.

"Okay, I'm at her desk. Give me a moment."

He gave the desk the once over, moved papers around, and said, "Nothing. No clue as to what they were up to."

"The police won't do anything. They haven't been gone long enough."

"Yeah, I know."

"Of course you do. Let me call Reece."

"Good luck with that."

"I'm not sure he and I are friends exactly, but we are friendly. And Em and I see him and his wife socially. So let me talk to him."

"Okay. And good luck."

Brandon put his phone in his pocket. Reece Sovern. *That'll be the day anything positive comes from him. But if anyone can, Harry's probably the man.*

# 61

## WEDNESDAY, JANUARY 15, 11:51 AM

Brandon's news was disturbing. Was Em off playing the Lone Ranger? I certainly hoped not. But knowing Em, I wasn't holding my breath.

The lunch crowd was arriving. Nevertheless, I told my phone to call Reece Sovern and on the third ring, I heard his voice.

"You have the most uncanny timing, Harry."

"How's that?"

"GJ and I just got back from talking with the realtor who found property for those Crimson Dawn whack jobs."

"Find out anything of interest?"

"Yeah. Their lawyer paid cash for the old Adolf Bauer farm."

"Cash? *That* is interesting."

"You called. What do you want? I'm kind of busy."

"I suppose you are. Em and Joyce are missing. They left Joyce's office a couple hours ago and haven't returned. Joyce even missed her appointment, and another realtor had to take it. I'm worried. Brandon's worried. And the realty staff are worried. What do you suggest?"

"No one knows where they went?"

"Nope. They didn't say a word where they were going."

"Can you give me a step-by-step account of their actions?"

"No. Brandon called to let me know, but gave no details. I'm assuming Em wanted to ask Joyce something, and then they left."

"Normally, I'd say no big deal. They'll show up. But given we have a serial killer out there and someone taking potshots at the Reverend, and a different perp, also offing ministers, this isn't sounding too good. Meet me at the real estate office in ten."

"Will do. Thanks."

I ended the call, told Jack where I was going, and headed for my car.

---

Reece's car wasn't visible when I pulled up in front of the reality office. Brandon's truck was, though, so I hurried inside.

He was sitting in the reception area and when he saw me, he said, "Read your text, so I'm waiting for our wonderful sergeant investigator."

"No fisticuffs between you two. He's here to help."

"About as helpful as a hemorrhoid."

The receptionist giggled.

"Give the guy a break, Brandon. He doesn't have the same skill and experience set as you, but that doesn't mean he's a nincompoop."

The former lawman gave me the squint-eye, shook his head, and said, "If you say so. And for the record, I think you're being generous."

"Generous?"

"Yeah, calling him a nincompoop."

I shook my head and sat next to him. A moment later, Reece and GJ arrived.

The sergeant investigator's black trench coat was open, revealing a wrinkled chocolate brown suit, white shirt, and no tie. A worn, dark brown fedora was on his head and scuffed brown oxfords were on his feet. The Zeppelin pipe was held at a jaunty angle.

By contrast, GJ wore a smart dark blue car coat over a navy blue jacket, cream-colored blouse, and navy blue slacks. She wore a pair of black Ugg boots on her feet. No hat covered her mannish hair cut.

Brandon and I stood when they entered.

Reece gave me a nod and said, "Harry," looked at Brandon for probably a good ten seconds and finally said, "Turner."

GJ ignored both of us.

"No word?" Reece asked.

"None," Brandon answered.

Reece nodded. "Where's her desk?"

"Already looked," Brandon said. "Nothing there."

"Okay. You looked. Mind if I look?"

Brandon rolled his eyes and said, "Follow me."

When we reached Joyce's desk, he said, "Here we are. Knock yourself out, Sovern."

Reece pushed his glasses back up to the top of his nose. He scanned the desktop, lowered himself into Joyce's chair and opened the drawers one by one, looking through the contents.

When he was finished, his eyes once again took in the top of the desk.

"Nothing there, is there, Sovern?" Brandon said.

Reece ignored him, while GJ gave Turner the evil eye.

After what seemed forever, Reece picked up the notepad lying by the desk phone and turned on Joyce's desk lamp. He studied the top sheet for a moment or two, then took a pencil out of his shirt pocket and began rubbing the lead over the top sheet of the pad.

Letters started to reveal themselves and a minute later, the detective held up the pad for Brandon and me to see.

"Well, well," I said.

GJ snorted a laugh. "Nothing here, hot shot, is there?"

Red suffused Brandon's face.

"I'll make a guess," our sergeant investigator said. "Ember came to visit Joyce. Probably to get info on real estate sales. Joyce gave her the information she gave me, and the two decided to head out to the farm."

Reece jotted the address down on two sheets of paper and handed one to Brandon and one to me. "In case you get lost. Follow me and we'll see if they're there."

The two investigators swept out of the office, leaving Brandon and me to follow.

I looked at the former cop. "Something wrong?"

"Yeah. Can't believe I missed that."

"Reece learned something in that FBI training."

"I guess he did. Let's go. The guy drives like a maniac."

# 62

## WEDNESDAY, JANUARY 15, 1:29 PM

Reece did indeed drive with a heavy foot, but his unmarked Tahoe was no match for my Alfa Romeo Giulia Quadrifolio. I followed him down the long driveway to the farmhouse. Brandon pulled in a minute later.

"You two are maniacs," he told us.

Reece shrugged. "Your girlfriend." An emerald green corona had replaced the Zeppelin cigar pipe.

"I hope you didn't unwrap that while driving," I said.

"Nope. GJ did it for me."

Brandon shook his head.

The four of us made three-sixty degree turns, taking in the emptiness, the isolation, the decay of the place.

"Doesn't look as though anyone has been here since the Great Depression," I said.

"There are quite a few tire tracks," GJ pointed out. "So someone's been here before us. And recently."

I watched the wind blow a tumbleweed or some similar plant across what was once the front yard.

"Betcha don't see this in New York City," Reece said to Brandon.

"Worse," was his reply.

Reece rolled his eyes.

I took out my phone and told it to call Em. There was no answer, and the call went to voicemail.

Hands on hips, Reece said, "Well, Turner, Joyce's car isn't here. What do you want to do?"

"Em's not answering her phone," I said.

Brandon tried calling Joyce, and after a minute said, "Voicemail."

GJ had wandered up to the front door. "Someone's been here. The lock is old, but there are fresh key insert marks." She then knocked on the door. When there was no reply, she pounded on it hard.

I found myself not wanting to have her fist connect with any part of my body.

"Doesn't appear to be anyone home," she said.

"I'm going to take a look at the outbuildings," I told the others.

"Good idea, Harry," Reece said.

There was a large barn. The weathered boards showed flecks of red paint, but were mostly a dirty gray.

Some distance away was a long building with large sliding doors. I guessed it to be a shed for farm equipment. On either side of the long building were two smaller square structures.

"I'll take the machine shed," Reece called out.

Brandon and GJ opted for the smaller buildings.

I moseyed over to the barn.

Something wasn't right with this picture. The New Order of the Crimson Dawn buys this run-down farm and pays cash for it. Ten months later, the only evidence someone's visited the place are tire tracks in the dirt and scratches around the front door key hole.

I stopped before the barn door. *Add to that one new padlock.*

Seeing I wouldn't get in by that door, I began a walk around the building. There were two other doors, and both were secured with new heavy duty padlocks.

*If they have everything locked up, I wonder if they also installed surveillance equipment?*

My walk around the barn complete, I voiced my concern about surveillance to the other three.

"Wouldn't be surprised if you're right, Harry," Brandon said.

"If there are cameras, it's too late for us to do anything about them now," Reece said.

"So where does that leave us?" I asked.

"Nowhere," Brandon said.

"Nothing we can do at this point," Reece added. "There's no proof Joyce and Ember were ever here."

---

The blonde woman with the Gibson Girl hairdo looked up from her phone. "It seems, Mrs. Faber, our women are missed."

"That it does, Mrs. Galt."

"What do you think we ought to do?"

"I think it's time we have one last sacrifice and then bid Magnolia Bluff adieu."

"But the full moon—"

"I know, Mrs. Galt. We will have to make up a special occasion for this sacrifice. One that doesn't require the full moon."

# 63

## WEDNESDAY, JANUARY 15, 5:08 PM

Graham Huston was eating chili with half a dozen saltine crackers crumbled into it.

I watched him chew and swallow a spoonful.

We were at a table in the Really Good. Estrelita and Jack had gone home. Miguel was cleaning up the kitchen, so it was ready for tomorrow. I'd told Graham about the farm.

He downed a second spoon of chili with crackers and said, "Something's definitely not right. You think Joyce and Ember are at the place?"

"I don't know. Would the Crimson Dawn hold them until the next full moon?"

Graham spooned his chili concoction and shrugged. "Maybe. Bird in the hand."

"The place was locked up tighter than a drum. Other than tire tracks and shiny new padlocks, it looked as though no one had been there in decades."

"Might not want vagrants taking over the buildings."

"Perhaps. I don't think that likely, though."

"It'll be dark soon. Want to take another look-see?"

After a moment's consideration, I nodded. "And perhaps add some surveillance of my own."

---

Reece Sovern was at his desk once again going over the evidence they'd collected thus far on the Full Moon Murders with GJ when his phone rang.

"Sovern."

"Brandon Turner, Sergeant."

"What do you want, Turner?"

"I want to help. My experience—"

"No dice. Captain Briggs wants no amateurs—"

"I'm a cop, Sovern, not an amateur."

"Were a cop. Correction, then. No *civilians* are to work on our cases. And I'm not getting a reprimand on your account."

"Okay, fine. I'll talk to Tommy."

"He's the one who hired Briggs, so good luck with that."

"If anything happens to Joyce—"

"Hold it right there, cowboy. Do you want to spend the night in jail?"

Reece looked at the phone and then dropped the handset in the cradle.

"Bastard hung up on me."

"Did he threaten you?" GJ asked.

"Started to. I understand where he's coming from. If it was Hetta..."

"Look, Sarge, Briggs is right on this. If one of these civilians gets hurt, they could sue us for some big bucks. He's looking out for the department."

"I suppose."

"I know you like Harry Thurgood and I don't understand why, but would you want him to get shot? It's not his place to be involved in a criminal investigation. It's our job and we need to buckle down and do it — and do it well."

"Yeah, you're right."

Reece understood Turner's frustration. He'd feel the same. But Turner had retired. He wasn't a cop anymore. He needed to let go and let the Magnolia Bluff cops and Burnet County deputies do their job.

He took in a bushel of air and let it out.

"What is it, Sarge?"

"I want to take another look at that place. You good with drones?"

"You bet! Haven't used those night vision models yet."

"Let's go after dark and give 'em a test drive."

# 64

## WEDNESDAY, JANUARY 15, 8:01 PM

I HELD my pencil flash in my mouth and attached the last of my tiny cameras to a tree. The lens focused on the barn door that faced towards the house.

"That was easy enough," Graham said. "This place sure looks deserted."

I slipped the flashlight into my pocket. "Doesn't it though? If it weren't for the stars, it would be dark as pitch."

"Reminds me of being out on patrol in rural Afghanistan."

"I can only imagine."

"I'm going to have to get some of these cameras."

"What for?"

"News, man. Just think of all the places I can put them and watch remotely. Then just write up real-time stories right from my desk chair."

"Scary thought, that."

He grabbed my arm and froze. Listening. Then yanked me behind the tree, saying in hushed tones, "Drone."

I listened and picked up the barely audible whirring of the rotors.

"Can you see it?" I asked.

"Funny, Harry. I can barely see you and you're right next to me."

"Who'd be flying a drone out here?"

"Crimson Dawn? Doing surveillance?"

"That would make sense."

"Especially if this is where those nutters off their victims. I mean, look, there's nothing out here. Nothing but empty land across the highway and on this side nothing but empty acres surrounding the house and outbuildings. Vacant land as far as you can see."

"Perfect place to kill your victims."

"Harry, if Joyce and Ember came out here, maybe they were captured by these nutters. It could even be that they're in the house."

That stopped me. What if they *were* here the entire time? And we idiots are wandering around while the women we are looking for are right under our noses. Oh, my God. Could it be?

"Graham, what would you think about a little breaking and entering?"

"Uh, I don't know, Harry. That might be going a bit too far. I understand. This is Ember we're talking about. But what if I'm wrong and we get caught?"

"Who's going to catch us? So far, we've seen no one."

"Are you forgetting that drone? Somebody's flying it. And we have no idea who it is."

"Speaking of the drone, where is it?"

"I don't know. I only hear it now and then, so it must be flying around the buildings."

"You must have really good hearing, because I don't hear the thing."

"There. Hear it?"

I focused. After a moment I said, "Yes. It's by the house, isn't it?"

"It was. But now it's coming this way."

"Crap."

"Just freeze."

I froze. The rotors became louder. And louder.

The thing must be right on the other side of the tree. Suddenly a bright light was shining on us and a tinny voice said, "This is the Magnolia Bluff police. Show yourselves."

# 65

## WEDNESDAY, JANUARY 15, 8:33 PM

GRAHAM and I looked at each other, shrugged, and stepped out from behind the tree into the drone's search light.

When I heard, "It's Huston and Thurgood, Sarge," I started chuckling.

Graham said, "As I live and breathe. Hey Sovern. GJ. Beautiful night, isn't it?"

"What are you two dumb asses—"

Sovern's voice replaced GJ's. "What the hell do you think you two are doing?"

"Surveillance," I said.

"You realize you're trespassing," GJ said.

"We knocked on the door," Graham lied.

"You wait right there. And don't move."

The drone settled to the ground and powered down.

"We're in the soup now," Graham said.

"Could very well be," I replied.

I tapped the flashlight on my phone and examined the little machine. Graham joined me and we were still checking it out when Reece's Tahoe drove into the driveway.

He stopped ten feet from us. GJ dashed out of the vehicle, scooped up the drone, and carried it back to the SUV.

"We weren't going to steal it," Graham said to her back.

Hands on hips, Reece said, "You two should not be out here. What were you doing?"

"I put up surveillance cameras to see if there's anything going on," I said.

"Huh. That might actually come in handy. Officially, though, I know nothing about this. Okay?"

"Gotcha," I said.

"You bet," Graham answered.

GJ rejoined us.

Reece removed the stogie from his mouth and pointed it at us. "And you'll share the information and not play Lone Ranger. Right?"

"You bet," I said.

Reece told GJ what I'd done. Her reaction was obscured by the darkness.

"Now you two get out of here," Reece ordered.

As Graham and I walked away, Reece called out, "And Harry, you might want to get a beater pickup if you insist on snooping. That fancy foreign job sticks out like a sore thumb."

GJ's derisive laugh rang out loudly on the night air.

# 66

## WEDNESDAY, JANUARY 15, 10:41 PM

On the way home, I dropped Graham off at Nell Walker's three-room boarding house over behind the high school football field where he rents a room.

Clara was waiting for me when I arrived, eager for news about Ember. Unfortunately, I had to disappoint her, for I had none.

I looked in on Max and Netty, kissing each of my sleeping children.

Gazing at the little sleepers, I knew I had to move heaven and earth to get their mother back. Hopefully, the surveillance cams were a step in the right direction.

The fireplace in the family room was cold and dark. I lay the kindling and logs, stuffed crumpled up paper underneath the andirons and lit the paper with a wooden kitchen match. In a moment, the paper was blazing, and the kindling began to smoke and then catch fire.

I mixed myself a Corpse Reviver No. 1, filled my pipe, lit it, and sat in my chair with my tablet.

Princess lay curled at my feet, and Wilbur was a tight little ball in Ember's chair.

Tapping the surveillance app, I saw what the little cameras saw: nothing. Nothing but the blackness of the night.

I puffed on my pipe, took a sip of my drink, and settled in for a long night of watching and waiting.

---

Mary Lou Fight took a sip of tea and set the cup down. The liquid, a bit too hot.

She had called the mayor to ask, demand actually, that the police make solving the murder of her minister their top priority.

The mayor assured her that the case was being pursued with due diligence, and that if she wanted details to call the chief of police.

Mary Lou had done one better: she'd had her driver take her down to the police station and talked to the chief in person.

And it was as she had suspected: they were focused on the so called Full Moon Murders.

"I do not understand why you are wasting time trying to solve the murders of these of out-of-towners when one of our own lies in the morgue crying out for justice," she'd said to Tommy Jager, MBPD police chief.

His response was not satisfactory. Something about tourism and business and all manner of things that made little sense.

She'd finally cut him off. "My minister is dead, and I demand you focus on finding his killer."

The chief had blinked at her and then said, "As far as I'm aware, Reverend Cole is still alive."

At the mention of Reverend Cole's name, Mary Lou stood and told him in no uncertain terms that Ms. Cole was not her pastor and if he didn't do something soon to apprehend the Reverend Humphrey's killer she'd be speaking with the governor.

Mary Lou picked up her teacup and drank tea. Aside from the incompetency of the police, something else bothered her:

Oralene's lack of grief at the passing of the Reverend Adelbert Humphrey.

*What is especially disconcerting is that she didn't even seem surprised at the news of his death. Then again, she sees it as a judgement from God. A death fitting for a Sodomite.*

Mary Lou shivered. Such a backward attitude. *The young woman still has a lot to learn,* she told herself.

What was even more troubling were the rumors she recalled that circulated during the trial of the young woman's brother. Rumors that hinted at Oralene being the one who had orchestrated the murder of her father and the Reston family's business manager.

Mary Lou set down her teacup and stared at the glowing embers in the fireplace. For the first time in her life, she wondered if she'd made an error in judgement.

*I just might have a problem on my hands. A big problem.*

---

Brandon had been at his wit's end ever since his unproductive phone call to Sovern. He'd done his best to keep Jason, Joyce's son, calm. But the longer the situation dragged on, the more not only worry but panic etched the boy's face. Even Olivia's pizza didn't help. The boy barely got down one slice before saying he wasn't hungry.

At that point, Brandon knew he had to do something.

"Tell you what, Jason, I'm going to go back to that farm."

"Can I go with you?"

"No. It might be dangerous. I need you to stay here with Max and if I'm not back in two hours, you need to call Harry Thurgood. Tell him I went out to the farm and ask him to call the police. Okay? I need you to do this."

"Okay, Brandon. If Mom comes home, I'll text."

"Deal."

Brandon cupped his dog's face. "Be a good boy, Max, and watch Jason and the house."

Then he gave Jason a side hug and headed out the door to his truck.

Once behind the wheel, he opened the glove box, took out his pistol, checked the magazine, and racked the slide to chamber a round.

# 67

## WEDNESDAY, JANUARY 15, 11:44 PM

HARRY HAD TAKEN two sips of his drink and a half dozen puffs on his pipe when the fun began.

He watched three pairs of headlights appear in the driveway of the old farm, and was surprised to observe a tall woman wearing a white Victorian-style dress get out of one of the cars and unlock the padlocks securing the doors of the machine shed.

But what made him almost drop his drink was the car in the shed illuminated by the three pairs of headlights. It was a dead ringer for Joyce's little sedan.

One by one, the cars pulled into the shed. Taillights winked out, interior lights came on, as doors opened and people exited the vehicles. That's when he spotted the second woman in white.

He counted six flashlights clustered around the tall woman who locked the padlocks securing the doors.

Harry zoomed in on the video to see if he could get a better view of the tall woman. The quality was too grainy for him to be sure, nevertheless he was willing to go out on a limb and say the woman was Augustinia Faber.

He set down his glass and pipe, dashed upstairs to his study, and unlocked the tall safe. From one shelf he took out a waistband holster and snub-nosed thirty-two caliber revolver, checked to make sure it was loaded, and pocketed a speedloader to have a reload available.

Next, he strapped on a belt and holster, chose his trusty S&W Model 19 .357 magnum revolver. The Border Patrol weapon of choice in days gone by. He made sure it was loaded and pocketed two speedloaders.

And to be ready for anything, he added a tactical knife, baton, night vision goggles, a flashlight, and took the cutlass off the wall.

*Don't know what I'll encounter, but as long as it isn't ten feet tall, has eight legs, and a thick shell, I think I'm good.*

He locked the safe, dashed downstairs, and on out to the garage.

As the Alfa Romeo slid out of the driveway and onto the street, he sent a text message to Clara informing her where he was going and that she'd see him when she saw him. Then he called Reece Sovern, knowing the police investigator would read him the riot act.

# 68

## THURSDAY, JANUARY 16, 12:27 AM

Reece Sovern was pissed.

He'd taken sixteen too long minutes to get dressed, put his service pistol in a shoulder holster, and a backup revolver in an ankle holster, and get out to his car.

In no uncertain terms, he told Harry to go home. But that was the equivalent of spitting into the wind.

He called Briggs and conveyed Harry's info. Briggs would waste no time mobilizing every available officer and probably call Sheriff Blanton for backup deputies.

Although the two would most likely get into a jurisdiction fight.

When his boss told him to "send that damn cowboy home," Reece laughed, told him "good luck with that, sir," and ended the call.

Given the time of night, Reece didn't bother with the siren. His lights, though, illumined the night to give warning that he was on a mission.

He pushed the SUV to the limit. When he was a mile from the farm, he cut the lights. He noticed Harry's fancy foreign car parked on the side of the road a hundred feet before the driveway, uttered a foul word, and when he reached the driveway, entered, and drove down its long, rutted length.

Three cars sat parked in front of the house. Reece recognized one vehicle as Brandon's truck. He shook his head, repeated the expletive, and muttered, "That's all I need: Turner out here."

Some distance to his right, he noticed a white light flashing on and off.

Reece stepped out of his vehicle and drew his pistol.

In a stage whisper he called out, "Is that you, Thurgood?"

The flashlight bobbed up and down.

"Of course it is," Reece muttered and quickened his pace.

When he was a few feet away from Harry Thurgood, he said, "What the hell are you wearing?" After a moment's pause, he continued, "You've got to be kidding me. A sword? Didn't you ever hear—"

"Yeah, I heard. And these are night vision goggles. They...," he held up the sword, "and this helped me dispatch the guy trying to get the jump on me."

"Is he dead?"

"Don't know. Cracked him on the head with the blunt back edge and he dropped to the ground like a lead balloon. Didn't make a sound."

Reece shook his head. "Did you bring a firearm to this fight, Jack Sparrow?"

"Captain Jack Sparrow. And yes, I did. Two, in fact."

"Where's Turner?"

"Don't know. Haven't seen him. Everyone else is in the barn."

"How many?"

"Eight. Could be ten. And I have a hunch Em and Joyce are in there as well."

"Guess the nutters aren't waiting for the next full moon."

"Looks like we made them accelerate the timetable."

"Back up should be here soon."

"Soon may not be soon enough. C'mon, Sarge, we have the element of surprise."

"Do you mind my asking, do you know how to use a firearm?"

"Six out of six in the bullseye at fifty feet."

"Of course. Why did I even bother to ask? Okay, Doc Holliday, let's go."

"After you, Wyatt."

Reece and Harry approached the barn.

"What's the best way in?"

"This is the only door that's unlocked. The two around back that go in the lower level are padlocked."

Reece looked at the large sliding door.

Harry said, "I'll push. You jump in and tell them they're under arrest. I'll be right behind you."

Reece nodded.

Harry set aside the sword and night vision goggles, grabbed hold of the door handle, and pulled.

As soon as the door opened enough for him to get through, Reece charged into the barn.

"Police! Everyone freeze."

For a moment, Reece observed a tableau that looked like something out of a horror movie.

On an altar made of wood lay a naked woman. Her arms and legs tied to stakes in the floor.

Surrounding the altar stood eight people in red robes, hoods obscured their faces.

At the head of the altar were two women clothed in white robes.

Four metal fire pits positioned outside the ring of people surrounding the altar provided the only light.

Reece became aware of Harry standing by his side. And as though in slow motion, he watched two of the hooded figures turn towards them, and as they did so they produced from under their robes sawed-off shotguns.

Reece fired a double tap and to his right, the roar of Harry's revolver was deafening.

Both robes were down, and the place erupted in pandemonium. People screaming and running everywhere.

Reece fired a shot to the barn roof and bellowed, "Police! Freeze."

Harry said, "My God, it's Augustinia and Hester."

"You know them?"

"Yes. Casually. Looks like I just became a bookstore owner."

"What?"

"Later. What do we do now?"

"Good question."

Before the two men stood Augustinia Faber, holding an obviously drugged Joyce Blackstone. She'd been taken off the altar in the pandemonium and was being used as a human shield. Hester Galt held a drugged Ember Cole before her. Off to the side, hands and feet tied, lay Brandon Turner, who seemed out of it.

The red robes had fled, save for the two lying on the floor.

Reece said, "Police and deputies have this place surrounded. Let the women go and surrender."

Augustinia smiled. "You have found out our little secret, Mr. Thurgood. It looks as though Mrs. Galt and I didn't keep close enough watch on you. Although we were hoping in time you and your pretty little wife would have joined us." She turned to Reece. "We are vrykolakes. Your weapons cannot hurt us."

Hester continued, "But we can kill these women." And to prove her point, she pressed the knife against Ember's throat until blood trickled down her neck. Then she licked the blade clean.

"What do you want?" Harry asked.

"What every living thing wants," Augustinia said, "to live."

Hester continued, "You let us live and we let these women and that man live."

Reece whispered to Harry, "What the hell is whatever they said they are?"

"I think they think they're vampires."

"You're kidding."

"Wish I was. I think the word they used to describe themselves is the Greek word for vampire, and that they believe they're vampires. Therefore, we can't kill them with firearms."

"Jesus. This place used to be so peaceful. And normal."

"What is your decision?" Augustinia asked.

"Why don't you just leave?" Harry said. "If we can't hurt you, just walk out of here."

"The women are insurance that you will let our initiates leave along with ourselves," Hester said.

"So, what do you need?" Reece asked.

"You and your fellows leave so we can get into our car with the women, and once we are confident you are not following or tracking us, you will get your women back."

"Alive?" Harry asked.

"Alive," Augustinia answered.

"I'll need to talk to my superior," Reece said.

"Then you had best hurry," Hester said, "for these women die in fifteen minutes if we do not have an agreement."

Harry whispered, "Do you think you can take out the redhead?"

"She's taller than Joyce. It'll be close. No margin for error. What about the blonde?"

"As you say, it'll be close. No room for error."

"I don't know, Harry. If we miss…"

"Then I guess we don't miss."

"Geez. I'd sure like to know your secrets. Talk about balls."

"Well, what do you say?"

"Keep an eye on them. I'll call Briggs."

When the call connected, before Reece could say a word, Briggs said, "What's the situation, Sergeant?"

Reece gave him the picture.

"I should've known that damn Thurgood would be there. I'm having a turf war with Blanton. But since that farm is more than a mile from town, it's technically his jurisdiction."

At that moment, Sheriff Buck Blanton's booming voice filled the barn. "Everyone freeze. Sovern, Thurgood, stand down."

A dozen deputies charged in and surrounded Reece, Harry, the women, and the hostages.

Reece shoved the phone into his pocket and watched the Crimson Dawn women look at each other. He raised his pistol. This was the moment of truth.

When the two women turned their heads to face him and Harry, smiles spread across their faces.

At the same time, he and Harry said, "Now," and pulled the triggers on their weapons.

# 69

## THURSDAY, JANUARY 16, 2:39 AM

AMBULANCES HAD COME AND GONE, taking Joyce Blackstone, Ember Cole, Brandon Turner, and Lucas Flynn (the fellow Harry had downed with his sword) to Burnet Medical Center.

Wiley Garrison, the coroner, was on his way to declare the dead to be truly dead.

Briggs and Blanton were arguing over the rightness or the wrongness of Reece and Harry shooting the women.

Earlier, Reece had answered Blanton's, "What the hell?", with, "They were going to cut Joyce's and Ember's throats. We had to shoot."

Reece once again looked at the bodies of the two women. His bullet had hit the redhead's forehead. Its exit had turned the upper third of the back of her head into a pulpy mush.

Harry's bullet had caught the blonde on her cheekbone and pretty much eliminated the right half of her head.

*I'm going to have to ask Harry what the hell he was shooting in that revolver of his.*

Blanton had confiscated the firearm, and Harry was at the hospital with Ember. The sheriff wasn't answering questions, and Harry was preoccupied with his wife. Reece would ask him later.

What mattered was that he and Harry had saved those women's lives. Both had the same gut reaction when they saw the ghastly smiles of the Galt and Faber women. They both knew that if they didn't shoot, Joyce and Ember would die.

Aside from the wannabe vampires, two of their followers were dead, one was in the hospital, four had been captured and were on their way to jail. Two were still at large.

Once Harry had identified the redhead and blonde, Briggs dispatched officers to their home and place of business.

It looked as though this case was closed. Next up, the Reverend Humphrey case. And that one was going to be just as difficult, if not more so, than the Full Moon Murder case.

*Who wanted the minister dead? A jilted lover? Someone who hated homosexual ministers? Someone who needed to get him out of the way? And out of the way for what?*

Reece shook his head. With no motive, he had no idea where to even begin looking. Other than to question half the town.

Briggs interrupted his thoughts. "This case should be a wrap. We didn't get the ring leaders—"

"Yes, we did." Reece interrupted and pointed to the bodies.

"Yes, they're dead. What I meant was we won't see them on trial and sent to prison, or even executed."

Reece closed his eyes, took off his glasses, and pinched his nose. He released his fingers, put his glasses back on, and goggled at his boss. "They were executed, in a manner of speaking, by Harry's and my bullets. Justice has been served and three lives saved, if we count Turner."

"Yes. I suppose you're right. Probably wouldn't have had to kill the perps if Thurgood wasn't involved."

"If it wasn't for Thurgood, we'd have three more corpses on our hands and the Faber and Galt women would've been on their way to another town. We stopped them with good police work *and* with the help of Harry Thurgood. Sir."

Reece turned and walked away, ignoring the spluttering of the captain.

He left the barn and walked out to his car.

The night sky was clear. The air was chill. There was no moon, but the stars were out in their millions.

He got into his SUV and chuckled. "Never in a million years would I have ever thought Harry and I would be friends. Seems as though that million years went by pretty quickly."

# 70

## THURSDAY, JANUARY 16, 2:39 AM

ASIDE FROM THE drug and the minor cut from the obsidian knife, the doctor said Em was fine. Physically. She may, however, experience some emotional trauma from the ordeal. That's something I'll have to watch for.

She's sleeping off the effects of the drug. The doctor said it was Phrancinol, which produces a hypnotic-like effect before the person slips off into sleep.

"Renders the person highly open to following suggestions," according to the doctor.

How Augustinia and Hester had gotten hold of the drug was a mystery, as it is still considered experimental.

I'm sitting in a chair next to the bed, holding Emmy's hand.

This is such a messed up world. Most days seem fine. And then it's crap like this, or her getting shot at, that remind you there are all manner of truly evil people out there planning and executing all manner of mayhem on people who are minding their own business and not bothering anyone.

I know that sounds unduly pessimistic. However, having lived in Magnolia Bluff for some time now I think I am justified in saying that whatever can happen will happen if enough time is allowed for it to happen. And we've seen it happen.

Who would've thought those two mildly kooky women were in fact horrendously evil monsters?

I conducted a quick search of the web and discovered all manner of interesting things about vrykolakes. While similar to a vampire, instead of drinking blood they eat flesh. Particularly the liver. And human livers are their favorite.

Somewhere, though, Augustinia and Hester got confused and added blood drinking to liver eating. At least I assume they were drinking blood. Why else would they exsanguinate their victims?

The fundamental existential question, though, is this: why do some people decide it is okay to intentionally kill their fellows?

I'm not a religious man. Nevertheless, I think all life is sacred.

I cringe when I see a tree cut down simply because "it's in the way." Trees don't have legal rights. But don't they have the moral right to life the same as we humans?

Or the cows that I end up eating? I mourn the death that takes place so that I may live. I welcome the day when we are able to grow meat in a lab so animals don't have to die that I might live.

Sure I could go vegetarian. But is the death of a carrot any less than that of a chicken?

Some, even most, would argue that a carrot isn't a sentient being. But we used to think cows were dumb beasts. Then we found out they have social structure. They problem solve. They have communication.

What's to say that we won't learn that carrots have a form of sentience we never thought possible?

Death is death.

And we the living live off of death.

Therefore, let's at least show some respect for the life that we take to sustain our own.

Presumably, Augustinia and Hester saw the rest of us as cattle. The blood, and in their case the liver, is the life. What was it that made them come to those beliefs? I regret their deaths as now I can't ask them. Mike Kurelek would have had a field day with them.

I know that private detective up in Minneapolis, Justinia Wright, had a case where the perp was a vampire lifestyler who went off the rails in the same manner as Hester and Augustinia. Murder and cannibalism. Take, eat, this is my body which is given for you. Consume the flesh and blood and take on the characteristics of the one eaten.

The Christian celebration of the eucharist is at heart a celebration as cannibalistic as that of the Aztec's human sacrifices. One literal and the other figurative. The cannibalistic language plain as day. Yet Christians for some reason don't see it. Buried in mystical ritual, I suppose. I'll have to ask Em.

With the Full Moon Murder case closed, I hope Reece can find out who tried to gun down my sweet bride.

My gut tells me he should look to Oralene. In my opinion, she has grade AA anti-social personality disorder. In plain English, she's a sociopath. And a killer.

"Hey Mister, what time it it?"

"You're awake." I got up out of the chair, leaned over, and kissed her.

"That was nice. What time is it? Can I go home?"

"It's quarter after three. The doc probably wants a bit more observation. The kidnappers gave you a pretty strong drug."

"How's Joyce?"

"She's okay."

"That's good. I thought I was going to die, Harry, and you know what was weird?"

"No. Tell me."

"I was okay with it. Not because I'd be with Jesus, but because my death would give them eternal life and I'd be eternal in them."

"That was the drug. Made you highly susceptible to believing them and following their instructions."

"I still feel sleepy."

"That's the stuff they gave you. You just need to sleep it off."

"Did you save me?"

"Yes."

"Thank you. I think I want to go away now. Someplace far away from here."

"Okay. Get some sleep and we'll talk about it."

"I love you, Mister."

"I love you, Rev."

She smiled a faint smile and nodded off.

Go away from here. At least for a time. That might not be a bad idea.

# 71

## SATURDAY, JANUARY 18, 8:11 AM

THE BELL over the door rang. I looked up and saw Reece Sovern enter the Really Good.

His eyes surveyed the place, and surprise was written large on his face. He stepped over to my table.

"What's up?" he asked. "I don't think I've ever seen it this busy." He sat in the chair across from me.

"What can I say? Murder is good for business. Even attempted murder when it involves Ember, Joyce, and Brandon."

Reece snorted at the mention of Brandon's name. "You know that arrogant son of a b doesn't believe I saved Joyce's life?"

"Oh, he probably does. Just doesn't want to admit it to you."

"Possible, I suppose."

"You know, he isn't that bad of a guy."

"So you keep telling me."

"Anyway, what can I do you for?"

"I wanted to let you know, and this is hush-hush."

"Mum's the word."

"I'm being shifted to a special assignment. Working for the State AG and Senate Ethics Committee. It's something I've been doing on the side for the past year. Now they want me full time for possibly up to another year."

"Congrats."

"Thanks. Also, Sergeant Palmer Kraus will be the temporary investigator in my absence. He's a good cop. Hopefully, he'll make headway on the murder of that minister from Ember's church and on who attempted to send her to the heavenly choir."

"I appreciate you telling me, but we may not be around much."

"Why's that?"

"Em feels she needs some time away."

"Can't blame her for that. She's gone through hell this month."

"It's been a month like no other. She's been a trooper, but the attempted murders have pushed her over the edge."

"Getting away from the Bluff is probably what the doctor should order." Reece stood. "Uh, if you do take off for parts unknown, mind keeping Hetta and me in the loop?"

I stood and offered my hand. He took it, and I said, "You bet, Sarge."

"Well, then, we'll see you when we see you."

He turned around and walked out the door.

I sat.

*Reece on special assignment with the State.* I shook my head and chuckled. *He's come a long way since that Crimson Hat affair. Who would have ever thought?*

# 72

## SATURDAY, JANUARY 18, 11:02 AM

Oralene Fight surveyed her handiwork. This was an entirely novel experience: to do the work of the Lord herself, rather than orchestrate it. And she had to admit she rather like the feeling.

She was no longer able to rely on her brother John-John to do her bidding. Plus, he was following in his father's footsteps. Footsteps that would lead him straight to hell.

This morning was a case in point. She had to chase some under age blonde harlot out of the building just so she could talk to her brother. It was a good thing her other brother, Lofton, was not in at the time.

The conversation did not go as she wanted it to. So when John-John turned his back on her, she struck him with the mallet she had brought. And then used the mallet to drive the tent peg through his skull.

*Jael lives in every woman, and will rise up in the face of weak men.*

After she made sure her brother would never cross her again, she left the building through the back door, drove over to the far side of the Reservoir, and threw the mallet into the water.

Only the harlot had seen her there, and she doubted the little fornicator would say anything. And if she did? Oralene smiled. The Lord always protects his servants.

---

Mary Lou Fight sat by the fire in the morning room drinking tea and eating croissants with orange marmalade. She enjoyed the yeasty fresh-baked smell of the bread and the sweet aroma of the marmalade.

There was a knock on the door frame, and Eliška entered.

"Did you find anything?" Mary Lou asked.

"Yes, ma'am. I found a journal."

"Where was it?"

"Inside a plastic bag in the toilet tank."

"Not bad. Although she will need to do better. Anything important?"

"I do not know. Many words I do not understand. I copied the pages for you and put the book back."

"Very good. Thank you, Eliška. There will be a bonus for you."

"Thank you, ma'am."

Eliška handed the photocopies to her mistress and departed.

Mary Lou drank tea and skimmed the few dozen pages.

There were all manner of obscure Biblical allusions. But one kept recurring, like a leitmotif: Jael freeing Israel by hammering a tent peg through Sisera's skull.

She set the papers aside, drank tea, put marmalade on the end of a croissant, and took a bite. She chewed and mulled over her adopted daughter's journal entries.

It was disturbing. The words indicated to Mary Lou that perhaps the girl was insane. If that was the case, she'd have to be dealt with. And probably sooner rather than later.

*She is a problem. A big problem. Mistakes cannot be allowed to linger.*

Mary Lou put the pages in the fire and put marmalade on her croissant.

# 73

## SUNDAY, JANUARY 19, 2:09 PM

I WAS DRIVING us back to Magnolia Bluff. We'd eaten our dinner at Oliver's in downtown Austin. The bishop insisted Ember take the rest of the month off to recuperate from her harrowing experience.

She'd been very quiet ever since receiving the bishop's "request" yesterday afternoon.

Finally, I decided the ice had to be broken.

"Okay, Miss Moody Blues, this is not the end of the world I'll have you know."

Her head turn towards me and a faint smile tugged at the corners of her mouth. "It's Missus," she said. "Did you forget?"

"Nope. Haven't forgotten. I'm glad, as Fergus would say, you're Mistress of the House Thurgood."

She let out a laugh. "That sounds like him."

"Do you want to talk about it? Might do some good."

She took in enough air to inflate the *Hindenburg* and let it out. Then began talking.

"I decided to see Joyce. I wanted a list of people who'd bought real estate in the area. It bugged the life out of me that Reece couldn't let us help him."

"So *you* decided to help *him*."

"Something like that. Anyway, when I told Joyce what I wanted, she said she could go one better. She could give me the information she'd given Reece. I told her that would be great. She wrote the address down and gave it to me. When I asked for directions, she volunteered to take me out there."

"That was nice of her."

"And it landed her in the soup."

I shrugged. "Stuff happens. You know that. Besides, doesn't your God control evil? Isn't that the implication in Job?"

"Yes, I suppose it is. But that's not the point, Harry. It's because of me she was almost killed."

"How so? You didn't make her go. She exercised her free will."

"Very funny, Mister. The point is, she wouldn't have volunteered to help me if I hadn't shown up."

"And if you hadn't shown up, the case might not have been solved and those two monsters would still be killing people."

When she didn't say anything, I prodded her. "So, what did you find when you got out to the farm?"

"A whole lot of nothing and a farmhouse with an open door."

"So curiosity got the better of you and you walked right in."

"Yes. And that's when they captured us. Those two women. They marched us upstairs, zip-tied our hands and feet, and injected us with some drug."

"Phrancinol. Makes you highly open to suggestion, like hypnosis, before putting you to sleep."

"They told us that our flesh and blood were sacred. That through eternal death we'd have eternal life, and they would have eternal life through our flesh and blood. When Joyce started to scream, the blonde woman shushed her and told her she was happy to give her life so that many would live forever. That she, Joyce, was doing a wonderful thing, and she was happy to do so."

"What about you?"

"They gave me the same spiel. And I believed them, Harry. That's what I can't get over. I wanted them to eat my flesh and drink my blood so they could live. I wanted it more than anything."

"That was the drug talking. Not you."

"I didn't think of you or the twins. Just them. I had to please them."

"It's over, Emmy. Over. Schedule time with Mike. The therapy will help."

When she again fell silent, I said, "Are you going to call Mike?"

"You know what I want?"

"No. Tell me."

"I want us to go far away from here. Far away and for a very long time."

# 74

## MONIKA HEARS

Monika Crow, Graham Huston's Gal Friday at the *Chronicle,* Magnolia Bluff's twice weekly newspaper, writes "Monika Hears" and it appears every Tuesday and Saturday, the days the paper comes out.

She hears a lot of things. Sometimes I wonder if she makes the stuff up. She swears she doesn't. Still…

In any event, here are a few things Monika has heard.

---

Monika hears our intrepid investigators at the MBPD, Reece Sovern and GJ Riggins, are on a potentially yearlong leave of absence. When asked what they will be doing, Chief Jager said he wasn't free to answer the question. Captain Briggs had a very colorful suggestion for what we could do with our microphone. Yankees.

This past week, Monika heard the police have several persons of interest connected to the horrific murder of Pastor John Reston of

Flaming Light Gospel Tabernacle. More information will be forthcoming.

Monika's also heard that Scarlett Hayden, the colorful owner of Hayden's Resort, has convinced her beau, Stanton Mirabeau Lauderbach, Esq., to take her on a round the world jet-setter vacation. Have gin bottle, will travel.

Monika hears the Fight family will be in Europe on an extended vacay, while the Cole-Thurgood household is taking a round the world cruise on a private charter sailing yacht. The cruise will take some three hundred days to complete. Sure must be nice to be rich.

# EPILOGUE

I THINK it is still morning. The sun is high in the brilliant blue sky. Em, Clara, and the twins, along with Princess (Wilbur refuses to leave the stateroom) are enjoying the ocean view seated amidships.

We've been cruising for 52 days on board the *Flying Mermaid,* a 132-foot brigantine.

Aside from Emmy and myself, Clara and the twins, Princess and Wilbur, the only other people on board are the captain and the crew. That's it. We have the yacht basically to ourselves. The crew is polite and does their very best to be invisible.

We left Galveston on the first of February and made our first stop in the Bahamas. From there, we sailed to Barbados, crossed the Atlantic to the Cape Verde Islands, and from there sailed on to Madeira.

We spent a week on Madeira. When the week was over, we set sail for the Mediterranean, stopping first at Palma in the Balearic Islands, followed by a short visit to Monaco.

We're now on our way to Genoa. I'm looking forward to visiting Italy. Italian cuisine is probably my favorite. And it's where the Roman Empire got its start.

I'm smoking my pipe, standing at the bow, and literally looking into our future. It is blue and sunny and warm.

Em seems to be doing well. We don't talk much about Magnolia Bluff.

On my part, I send the periodic text to Reece. I'm in more regular contact with Graham and Miguel. Miguel, Jack, and Estrelita are running the Really Good until we get back.

It must sound crazy, but I'm looking forward to getting back home. And Magnolia Bluff is home. It is where I hang my hat and lay my head. It's where my friends are. And it's where my life is.

Magnolia Bluff. That quiet little family friendly town in the Texas Hill Country. The best place to call home. Even if murder does wait in the wings.

# AFTERWORD

I hope you enjoyed *Death by Moonlight.*

If you did, please leave a review where you bought the book and on your favorite social media sites. Your review is like word of mouth advertising. And it is pure gold.

**Enter my World**

Enter my world and you'll find that murder was never so good. Just click, tap, or scan the QR code below.

There's nothing like a good old-fashioned slow burn murder mystery. The quirky characters. The eccentric sleuth. The bumbling police detectives. The nefarious villain. And of course, the leisurely pacing until we reach the exciting climax.

If you are new to the Magnolia Bluff Crime Chronicles, then *Death By Moonlight* is an excellent entry point into the series and into my world.

In addition to my books in the Magnolia Bluff Crime Chronicles, I write the Justinia Wright Private Investigator Mysteries, which are an homage to Nero Wolfe and Archie Goodwin. You'll discover exciting stories, eccentric and quirky characters, and wicked killers. And if you like Magnolia Bluff, you're sure to like Justinia Wright's Minneapolis.

So just click, tap, or scan the QR code to enter my exciting world of mystery and mayhem. You will get a free copy of *Vampire House and Other Early Cases of Justinia Wright, PI* and you'll get my monthly email of news and curated contact. The game is a foot!

# ABOUT THE UNDERGROUND AUTHORS AND THE MAGNOLIA BLUFF CRIME CHRONICLES

**A Co-op of Authors**

The late Caleb Pirtle III organized the Authors Marketing Cooperative in mid-2020. The purpose was to harness the collective reach of a dozen authors to promote each other's books.

But writers like to write and it didn't take long for the co-op to come up with the idea to put together a member collection of short stories to aid the joint marketing efforts.

*Beyond the Sea: Stories from the Underground* was published in April 2021. (Pick up a copy from Amazon) And with the publication of the story collection, the co-op began calling itself the Underground Authors.

Little did the authors realize that with the publication of *Beyond the Sea* things were about to change and change in a way they couldn't even imagine.

**Magnolia Bluff**

In May 2021, coming back from an online writers conference, CW Hawes proposed that the Underground Authors write a multi-author series. After a flurry of emails that sketched out the broad picture, the important landmarks and the main characters each writer would use in his or her books, the Magnolia Bluff Crime Chronicles was born.

The series revolves around the goings on in the small (fictional) Texas Hill Country town of Magnolia Bluff. The lives, loves, and deaths that happen in our town are chronicled by each author. A dozen different perspectives on life in Magnolia Bluff, Texas. That beautiful and peaceful little town on the shore of Burnet Reservoir, where murder waits in the wings.

We are now in our fourth year and Magnolia Bluff has taken on a life of its own. For the writers and readers, the town has become a real place.

We are amazed at the wonderful reception the series has received. It's exciting to know that we have something that is a little bit unique in the world of crime fiction.

I hope you enjoyed this chapter in the ongoing saga that is Magnolia Bluff. If this is your first visit, I hope you come back for more. And if you are a return visitor, thank you for once again making the trip to our favorite small town.

All the best, and be sure to look behind you.

# COMING TO MAGNOLIA BLUFF IN FEBRUARY

Coming out towards the end of February will be *Something's Fishy in Magnolia Bluff* by KD McNiven. And if I know Ms. McNiven, I know this will be one exciting thrill read. I can't wait.

And to whet our appetite, below is a sample of *Something's Fishy in Magnolia Bluff*. Enjoy!

"We don't want any stinking fish near our place!" Randy Scolfield yelled. His anger rose like a room thermostat on a hot day. With a white-knuckled grip on his chair, he listened to the cacophony of outraged voices that followed. Tensions mounted by the minute at the county commissioners' meeting. Because of the unique circumstances and sensitivity surrounding tonight's topic, they met at the VFW Hall on the outskirts of Magnolia Bluff, Texas. Fiery exchanges were not uncommon during these meetings. This one would not be the last.

Deputy Detective Madeline (Maddy) Dawson Baker twisted her head to the side, strands of brown hair brushing over her shoulder to see her husband John's reaction. She noted his eyes flicking from Randy to Soren Royal like an exhilarating tennis match. No one scored in this round.

Soren quickly pivoted to defend himself. "Look, I've already received the permit to raise Mozambique Tilapia. I've every right to farm them. I've done extensive studies on raising them, and I don't see why any of you have a problem with it!" Soren gritted his teeth. A scowl pinched his already deeply chiseled face.

"I've studied the law of nuisance," Piper Wainright said. "Your neighbors haven't bought into this lame idea you've cooked up. Maybe you should consider those around you who don't favor this project."

"Hear, hear!" A voice rang through the thickly charged atmosphere, crackling like the Fourth of July fireworks.

Elaina Parker leaped to her feet, wagging her finger in the air at Soren. "We entertain weekly. Our backyard is one of the most beautiful on the outskirts of Magnolia Bluff, so all our neighbors tell us. Not only will your fish farm carry the stench of an algae slime pit, but it will also be unsightly. I don't want my guests exposed to such an eyesore."

"Put up a fence!" Soren ground out, having lost any empathy.

Elegantly dressed, Tiffany Graceson took to her feet—no surprise to those in attendance. She poked her nose into any scrap of potential gossip, and this meeting was winding up as a doozy of a tongue-waggle. She'd already vowed to take the fierce objections to online podcasters about the juicy goings-on in Magnolia Bluff. "Why should Elaina have to put up a fence when it's your project?"

"Fine! I'll see to it. I'll build a fence so her guests don't get offended." Soren swiped the sweat from his brow.

"A fence won't cure the smell!" Elaina shouted. "What will happen when an unsuspecting child wanders onto your property and tumbles in?"

"Heavens, woman. You can't stop yourself, can you?" Soren threw his hands in the air, frustration mounting with every objection.

County commissioner, Jay Holcomb, pounded his gavel.

"Let's settle down now. Don't get yourselves worked up. Let's hear Soren out."

The cord in Soren's neck swelled, fighting to control his temper. Most of his neighbors didn't approve of him starting a fish farm. However, the meeting provided hope for eventually resolving their conflicts. However, it became clear as the discussion progressed that it only escalated the situation since last month's meeting. Soren pulled out as much sound reasoning as possible, though nothing appeared to satisfy the group. They were determined to excoriate him harshly, branding him a lunatic for his outlandish endeavor.

"I said I'd build a fence. That should keep children from coming onto my property. The fish will benefit the community." Soren continued his defense of the farm in a firm Danish accent.

"How do you figure?" shouted Randy.

"Aquaculture increases food production. It lends itself to helping feed the poor. You must agree, plenty of people could use a good meal these days. Tilapia is suitable for pickling and drying and is chock full of nutrients. The fish also feed on algae, plant-based foods, so they don't endanger other species."

No longer able to keep his unrestrained emotions in check, Randy toppled his chair as he stormed forward, closing the gap between himself and Soren. He leaned in, his face mere inches from Soren's. His eyes blazed with fury. "What happens when the river breaches and the tilapia gets swept into Burnett Reservoir and contaminates its eco-system? Then what?" Randy poked his finger in Soren's chest provocatively, knocking him off balance.

"Order! Order!" Jay called out, slamming the gavel repeatedly against the sound block.

Soren could not maintain his footing and toppled over Gill Simmons, the owner of O'Gara's bar, who sat beside him when everything disintegrated like rotting compost. Arms and legs flailed as Soren scrambled from Gill's lap, angered beyond reason. Without considering his actions, Soren swung wildly and clipped Randy's jaw.

Randy's head snapped to the side, and he staggered. Shaking it off, he placed his focus back on Soren, nostrils flaring. He snorted like a raging bull, set his feet, and raised both fists to challenge Soren.

The scene, which had rapidly taken a dangerous shift, brought Maddy out of her chair. She lunged forward to clutch Soren's arm, anticipating an out-and-out brawl.

Gill leaped forward to intervene as well. It seemed like the logical thing to do until Randy retaliated by pushing Soren into him. He stumbled backward, landing on Father Lee, leader of Christ the King Church, who'd rode out to the meeting with Gill to listen in on what all the hubbub was about. Unfortunately, he received first-hand knowledge when Gill's body crashed on top of him.

Though shaken by the unsatisfactory denouement, Father Lee eased Gill off of him to regain his composure, stunned by the bombshell of emotions.

Unfazed, Gill snagged a firm hold on Randy's arm, though an inflamed Randy, unwilling to yield, yanked free from his grasp and bounded forward like a frantic jackrabbit, swinging uncontrollably. Regrettably, Maddy stood too close and took a right hook to the cheek.

Maddy did her best to recover from the blow and reached into her back jeans pocket to snag a zip tie, a habit she'd acquired for times like this. She struggled against his thrashing but finally bound Randy's wrists, then led him to the side of the room.

She happily embraced Gill and John's intervention amidst the mayhem. Fortunately for Gill, his girlfriend had opted to stay home, or it could easily have been Fleur Beauchamp who took the brunt of Gill being thrust roughly into her. Thank goodness for small mercies, Maddy ruminated.

During the ruckus, Maddy had spotted her husband's quick

reaction. It was apparent to her he was stunned by how the meeting had gotten so outlandishly chaotic, and he'd barreled forward to assist her by clamping both arms around Soren's middle to restrain him. Soren's arms had flailed like a Dutch windmill as he tried to go after Randy, but he was no match for John, an ex-football star, who had no intention of loosening his hold on Soren until he calmed down.

"You two are going to the station to cool off. Hopefully, you'll act like mature adults in the future," said Maddy. She glanced over at Gill, who was brushing off his blue jeans and chambray shirt from the scuffle. Although they lived within the city, he and Father Lee made an effort to stay informed about any amendments occurring in the county, which may or may not affect them in the future.

"Are you okay, Gill?"

"Better than you, I'd say." His gaze flicked appraisingly where Randy had clipped her.

"I'm fine. Dealt with worse," Maddy said. "I hope things settle down before this situation gets more volatile."

Father Lee joined them, wearing a friendly smile as usual. His eyes leveled on Maddy. "You appear to be all right after getting popped, thankfully. This was not what one would expect at a community meeting."

"Yes, wilder than I'd foreseen, too. Like I told Gill, I'll sport a bruise for a few days. It could've been much worse. Thanks for your concern. What about you?"

Father Lee grinned widely. "Ah, Gill's a lightweight. I'm good. My shoulder took a good slamming, but I'll put a hot pad on it this evening and it should be okay by morning. Nothing too serious."

"Catch you later. Thank you for lending a hand. It could have escalated into a riot."

"No problem, Maddy. Take care," said Gill.

Maddy couldn't believe the meeting had taken on such a disorderly turn. The way Commissioner Sandra Clemons acted,

Maddy could almost swear the lady was about to jump out of her chair and join the rowdy conflict like a few other Magnolia Bluff residents who opposed Soren's tilapia farm. Wildfire sparked in Sandra's eyes. Her white-knuckled grip on the table's edge was the only thing holding her back. Who could have predicted the topic of a fish farm could cause such a dramatic climax? Not Maddy, for one.

Maddy called the Burnet County Sheriff's Department. Given that she was off duty, and they had walked from their house to the meeting hall, she needed to report the incident.

"Sheriff Buck. We could use your help about now."

"What's up, Dawson, or now Baker? Aren't you still supposed to be on your honeymoon?"

"We can discuss that later. Situations at the IOOF hall escalated. A bit of a fracas ensued. I restrained Randy. John is holding onto Soren Royal. I thought maybe a few hours behind bars might cool them down. We walked here from the ranch, so I have no way of hauling them in." Maddy heard a deep-throated chuckle on the other end.

"A couple of hotheads, huh? I'll be right over," Buck said. "Tell them if they misbehave any further, I'll bust their chops."

No one had ever accused Buck of being politically correct. Regardless, he was always fair in his dealings with law-breakers.

Her life took a turn after being hired by Buck, not solely because of the job. She shifted her gaze over to where John stood and smiled. When things were at their worst, he'd reentered her life. Eight months later, they walked down the aisle to share their vows. She glanced at the sparkling ring on her finger. Nothing could surpass this.

# BOOKS BY CW HAWES

CW is a multi-genre author. The books below are portals to his many exciting worlds. And no AI was used in the writing of these books.

**Justinia Wright Private Investigator Mysteries**

Justinia Wright is the PI with panache. These slow burn mysteries, written in homage to Rex Stout's Nero Wolfe, are sure to satisfy your craving for intriguing puzzles, quirky characters, and wise-cracking humor.

*Vampire House and Other Early Cases of Justinia Wright, PI*

*Festival of Death*

*Trio in Death-Sharp Minor*

*But Jesus Never Wept*

*The Conspiracy Game*

*A Nest of Spies*

*When Friends Must Die*

*Death Makes a House Call*

*To Right a Wrong*

*The Nine Deadly Dolls*

*Ripples on the Pond*

*Christmas with the Wrights*

*Minneapolis's Finest*

*Jack in the Box*

*Sauerkraut Days*

*Justinia Wright Private Investigator Omnibus Edition*

**Magnolia Bluff Crime Chronicles**

Tense slow burn mysteries set in our favorite town in the Texas Hill

Country.

*Death Wears a Crimson Hat*

*Ten Million Ways to Die*

*Who Mourns Elektra?*

*Death by Moonlight*

**Pierce Mostyn Paranormal Investigations**

The X-Files meets Cthulhu. Pierce Mostyn does battle with inter-dimensional monsters bent on the destruction of humanity.

*Nightmare in Agate Bay*

*Stairway to Hell*

*Terror in the Shadows*

*Van Dyne's Vampires*

*The Medusa Ritual*

*Demons in the Dunes*

*Van Dyne's Zuvembies*

*In the Shadow of the Mountains of Madness*

**The Rocheport Saga**

A post-apocalyptic adventure series in the style of cozy catastrophes such as *Earth Abides* and *Day of the Triffids.* Join Bill Arthur as he strives to build a new and better world on the ashes of the old.

*The Morning Star*

*The Shining City*

*The Divided City*

*The Troubled City*

*By Leaps and Bounds*

*Freedom's Freehold*

*Take to the Sky*

**Decopunk**

Alternative history adventures in a world where World War II never happened and swing is still king.

From the Files of Lady Dru Drummond

*The Moscow Affair*

*The Golden Fleece Affair*

Rand Hart Adventures

*Rand Hart and the Pajama Putsch*

**Tales of the Macabre**

For the horror lover in you.

*Do One Thing For Me*

*Metamorphosis*

*What the Next Day Brings*

*Ancient History*

**Anthologies**

Enjoy CW's stories in these short story collections.

*The Phantom Games*

*Beyond the Sea*

*Overmorrow*

*Arachnapocalypse! The Anthology*

*Once Upon a WolfPack*

You can find all of CW's books at Amazon. Just tap, click, or scan the QR code.

## ABOUT CW HAWES

CW Hawes is a multi-genre author because he's a multi-genre reader.

He's penned works in a variety of genres, including:

The Justinia Wright Private Investigator Mysteries

Four novels in the Magnolia Bluff Crime Chronicles series

The Rocheport Saga: A Post-Apocalyptic Steam-Powered Future

The Pierce Mostyn Paranormal Investigations

And assorted alternative history / decopunk, science fiction, and horror offerings.

CW is enjoying his retirement writing, walking, playing chess, and enjoying the art of doing nothing.

He hasn't met a doughnut or a pizza he doesn't like, is something of a tea snob, and rocks out to Handel and Vaughan Williams.

You can reach him at his website, on X, and also Facebook. Just tap, click, or scan the QR codes below.

His website:

His X account:

His Facebook page:

Jennifer lives in Texas with her husband, two children, and a menagerie of demanding cats, dogs, fish, and shrimp.

Her books can be found on Amazon, B&N, Siren.com and other fine e-retailers.

www.ingramcontent.com/pod-product-compliance
Lightning Source LLC
Chambersburg PA
CBHW072321280626
47159CB00027B/137
* 9 7 8 1 9 4 0 0 6 1 0 3 0 *

www.ingramcontent.com/pod-product-compliance
Lightning Source LLC
Chambersburg PA
CBHW070848250626
47159CB00003B/989
*9781942376453*